Believe the unbelievable.

The Orb

By

Estelle Godsman

In what form will the messiah appear?

Chapter 1

Holly stirs in her sleep. A voice is calling her name, soft and gentle like a breeze.

"Holllleeeee. Holllleeeee."

A ball of light hovers just beyond her reach… teasing her. The ball drifts away and she follows it through shadowy tunnels of green, silver and gold. It remains tantalisingly out of reach. Tendrils of silvery green mist flow from the ball and curl themselves around her shoulders. She tenses. Hands grab her from behind.

"Aaagh! Get away! Get off me!

Suddenly she is wide awake as her bedclothes are jerked off. Her ten year old brother's face looms over hers.

She shrieks, "Get away!"

Max grins and gleefully dances out of reach. Holly grabs the bed clothes and buries herself under them.

"Leave me alone."

"Grandpa says we're walking in five minutes,"

Holly groans. She'd much rather stay in bed and read.

"Awesome!" exclaims Max. "Wow! That is so awesome."

Holly surfaces. Max is staring out the window. Holly kneels up. A soft silvery green mist is curling its way in and out of the bush that separates her Grandparents' house from the beach. A chill runs across her skin.

Max races from the room.

"Five minutes," he yells.

Holly can hear him excitedly calling to Carla, her younger sister, as he bounds down the stairs.

"Carla! You've got to see this!"

Holly falls back on the bed but the soft voice of her dream is calling her. She gets up and stands at the window. The silvery green mist flows from the bush and crosses the road into the garden. It encompasses Grandpa and Carla who are waiting, with the two dogs, at the gate. Fingers of the mist weave their way through the garden towards her window. She stands frozen.

A gentle tap on her door breaks the spell.

"'Morning Holly. May I come in?"

Holly turns momentarily as her Nanna enters. She joins Holly at the window and gives her a brief hug. She is only slightly taller than fourteen year old Holly and not much bigger. She measures herself against her granddaughter.

"I'm still winning," she smiles.

Holly grins. "But I'm catching you," she teases in return. She turns back to the window. Max has joined Carla and Grandpa at the gate. The mist is suspended between the trees and shrubs.

"What is it?" asks Nanna.

"A strange mist…" Holly shudders.

Nanna watches it carefully.

"Grandpa waves to them and calls out. "Three minutes."

"Coming." Replies Nanna.

"You coming, Holl?"

Holly hesitates and looks out at the mist. She nods.

"It's friendly, you know," Nanna assures her. "See you in three minutes," she smiles, emphasising the three. Her husband is rather particular about time. "Remember to lock the door. I've got the key,"

As she leaves, Nanna notices Holly's i-Pod on the drawers.

"It might be a good idea to bring your i-Pod too," she suggests. Holly frowns. Why would she need her i-Pod? Friendly? How can a mist be friendly? Nanna sometimes says strange things. Besides drawing and painting, Nanna practises and teaches hypnosis, reiki, and meditation. Holly's dad often teases her by asking 'how's the raking going or are there any more nudes in the bedroom yet? He thinks he's funny. Nanna just smiles her amused smile. She's always very quiet and calm. Nanna gave him Reiki once, when he cut off his finger. She says he really 'got it' but he pretends he didn't. She gave Holly Reiki too. It was like floating in a sea of calm.

Holly takes another look through the window. She gasps. The mist is curling its way through the glass. It gently touches her on the arm. She hears the dream voice calling….

"Holllleeeee. Holllleeeee."

"Wow!"

Max and Carla turn in surprise as Holly joins them at the gate.

"A new record!" jokes Max.

Holly grimaces at them and says hello to the two dogs, Champ and Curly.

"Did you see the mist?" asks Carla. "It's sort of creepy. Like something out of one of your books.

Holly nods. She nervously looks around.

"It's gone back to the bush", says Max. "It's like it's waiting for us."

Holly looks across the road and sure enough the silvery green mist is there drifting between the gum trees and bushes… waiting for them… for her?

"Come on then. Lets get going", suggests Grandpa. "Or it'll be lunch time and not breakfast when we get back."

He opens the gate. Max, Carla and the dogs bolt across the gravel road to the bush-lined track that leads to the beach. Grandpa hurries to catch up with them.

"Don't worry about the traffic," mutters Holly under her breath. Nanna gives her, her amused smile, as they cross the road and enter the narrow, windy, sandy track. Holly stays close to Nanna. The bracken along the edge of the track is taller than them. It forms a barrier between the track and the rest of the bush. The mist keeps its distance, flickering green, silver and gold in the early morning sunlight.

Holly is glad when the track finally widens and opens onto the beach. Apart from themselves and a few gulls, the beach is empty. The soft white sand stretches before them. The sea is very calm, shining like a sheet of glass, still as a lake. The tide is so far out that the sandbank, between the inner and outer channel, is exposed. The morning sun catches the ripples of water as they break on its surface. The dogs are chasing each other through the shallows and Grandpa is leisurely making his way to the water's edge. Max and Carla have found some sea snail egg jellies and are throwing them at each other. It looks like another beautiful, normal day. Nanna and Holly take off their shoes and leave them with the other shoes at the end of the track. The sand is cool between the toes.

"Race you to Grandpa!" says Nanna suddenly, catching Holly unawares. She takes off with Holly in hot pursuit. Nanna stops, just in time to avoid a collision with her husband.

"I can still beat you." she laughs as Holly charges in.

"Yes, but you had a start," puffs Holly.

"Ugh, she gasps, as a couple of soft, wet, slimy jellies hit her in the neck. Max and Carla laugh. Holly takes off after them.

The battle is in full swing, Max and Carla versus Holly and Grandpa. Nanna cheers from the sidelines. "Come on Henry! Go Holly! Look out Carla. Max's right behind you."

Carla turns and receives a handful of jelly full in the face.

"What the....? You're supposed to be on my side."

Max doubles with laughter.

Carla joins forces with Holly and Grandpa. They bombard Max, forcing him towards the water.

Suddenly there is a loud commotion from the dogs. They all stop and turn to see what it's about. Both dogs, shackles up, are barking furiously at something in the wet sand, further up the beach.

Grandpa calls them but they ignore him. The group hurries along the beach. An amazing sight greets them. Carla and Grandpa hold back the dogs. They all stand and watch in bewilderment as several mounds, about a metre apart, rise from the sand. They look like small volcanoes. They grow until they're about half a metre high. Around them dark patterns, like tree silhouettes, are sketched in the sand.

"What are they, Grandpa?" whispers Carla.

"I don't know." he whispers back.

"Look! The middle one!" whispers Max urgently.

They edge closer. What looks like a glass ball, the size of a large grapefruit, rises from the centre of the mound. The sunlight catches its surface and is reflected onto Holly who is using the camera on her ipod. She gasps and moves further back, behind Nanna.

Carla and Max creep forward.

"Careful," warns Grandpa.

"It's okay Henry," says Nanna. "Good girl, Holly," she adds pointing to the ipod.

Grandpa gives her a curious look.

"Can we have it?" asks Max excitedly. As he moves closer, the ball retreats back into the mound.

"It doesn't seem to like you, Max," laughs Nanna.

"Don't blame it", mutters Holly under her breath.

Carla pulls Max back and the ball rises again.

"You try then smartie!" Max shoves Carla towards the ball. She shrieks and the ball moves back into the sand. She scampers back. Once more the ball rises and the sunlight is reflected off it, onto Holly.

"I think it likes you, Holly," says Nanna

"No way." Holly steps further back.

"You try Em," suggests Grandpa.

Holly continues to take photos as Nanna moves slowly towards the ball. It sparkles in the light. The group follows closely behind her, holding their breaths. She bends down and carefully scoops her hands into the mound and underneath it. It's cool and smooth to touch. It's quite light. She gently lifts it from the mound of sand and holds it up. They all let go of their breath. Grandpa, Max and Carla gather around her. Holly and the dogs keep their distance. The interior is a swirling mass of silver and green.

"It's like the silvery green mist is inside it," murmurs Carla.

"Wow. Cool!" exclaims Max. "Can I touch it? He reaches out to touch the ball. Nanna almost drops the ball as sparks suddenly erupt from it.

"Phew!" Max draws back.

Holly laughs. "It certainly doesn't like you."

Max makes a face and asks.

"Can we take it home?"

"No! Just leave it here where it belongs."

They all turn to look at Holly, surprised by the tension in her voice. Grandpa moves to her side and gives her a quick hug.

"It's just a glass ball," he says.

"Just a glass ball... that just happens to emerge all by itself, out of a sand mound, that just happens to rise, all by itself, out of the sand... I don't think so." Holly surprises herself and feels her face go red.

Carla stares at her in amazement.

"You're scared," she says. "It's just like all those scary books you read and you're not frightened of them."

"I'm not scared." She glares at her sister.

"You are so," declares Carla. "Come closer if you're so brave." Carla pulls Holly's arm but lets go as Nanna gives her a frown. Goaded by Carla's accusation, Holly takes a deep breath and steps forward to stand next to Nanna and the ball. The ball glows brightly. She tentatively reaches forward to touch it with the tip of her fingers but draws back. "No!" just put it back. "Pleeeease Nanna."

Nanna hesitates.

The mist inside the ball pulsates. A curious hum, like a mantra fills the air. Grandpa rubs his ears.

"Am I hearing things or what...?"

"I can hear it too!" exclaim Carla and Max together.

"Me too," says Nanna. "Can you Holly?"

Holly nods. She shrinks back behind Nanna, as the surreal sound echoes softly around them. The two dogs whimper softly and drop to the sand, their eyes and ears alert. No one moves.

"I know this sounds ridiculous but I think it's saying something." Grandpa's voice is hushed and unsure. They all listen intently trying to catch the words.

Nanna suddenly turns to Holly in the same instant of awareness. The both hear the soft call of her name.

"Hollllleeeee."

"It's calling you, Holly," says Nanna in wonder. "It wants you."

"No!" shrieks Holly. "I don't want it."

She bursts into tears, turns and runs back up the beach. The dogs race after her. Grandpa makes a move to follow her but Nanna shakes her head.

"Let her go. She'll be okay. The dogs are with her."

Carla picks up Holly's ipod that she'd dropped in her rush to escape.

"Do you think we should put it back?" asks Grandpa, indicating the ball.

"No." chorus Max and Carla together.

Nanna and Grandpa exchange glances, both uncertain.

Suddenly the roar of crashing water reverberates along the beach.

Startled, they all turn quickly as, from nowhere, a series of waves

erupts from the calm sea and charges along the water's edge

towards them, like a Mexican Wave at a football match. They

frantically scramble up the beach to escape but it swallows them

up to their thighs. They are soaked. They stand together, a sodden

gathering, watching the wave roll further down the beach.

As quickly as it came, the wave disappears back into the sea.

"Well we can't put it back now," declares Max. He points.

They stare in disbelief. Behind them, the sand is totally flat. There

is no sign of the mounds. The pattern of trees in the sand has

dissolved. It's as if they never existed.

"It looks like Max is right," says Grandpa.

"We can have it then?" whispers Max eagerly. Nanna nods. Max

punches the air with a clenched fist of victory.

"Yes!"

Carla feels a tingling in her skin. She looks back towards the

bush. She gasps. The silvery green mist from the bush is flowing

across the sand towards them. It wraps itself around them all, in a

soft blanket of stillness. No-one speaks. Moments pass and they

are held motionless. Even Max is captured by the silence and

peace. Then the mist is drawn into the glass ball, that's still firmly

held in Nanna's hands and the brightness of the day is restored. It

takes seconds before they are fully back in the present moment.

Even Nanna is lost for an explanation. She studies the glass ball.

There is something different about it. The silvery, green mist

seems denser. There is a ribbon of gold opening a winding path,

revealing a tantalising glimpse of… She can't quite see… Then

it's as before, just filled with the silvery, green mist.

"Breakfast time," she announces. "Come on."

She brightly leads the way back to their track at the edge of the

beach. The rest of the family follow, each of them bursting with

questions. Carla takes one last photo of the beach, a model of

normality. They collect their shoes and make their way back

through the bush. Bright shafts of sunlight shine on them as they climb the track home. There is no sign of the mist.

They cross the road to the house and Grandpa opens the gate. Holly is sitting on the swing, the dogs at her feet. She stares horrified at the ball in Nanna's hands.

"You didn't put it back?"

"We couldn't."

Nanna gently explains what had happened. Grandpa puts his arms around Holly.

"It'll be all right," he assures her.

They follow Nanna along the paved path to the back door.

"Could you please hold this for me? I have to get the key out of my pocket."

She holds the ball out. Holly draws back. Max and Carla make a grab for it. Max has it but Carla snatches it from his hands. The ball slips in Nanna's hands. She tries to grab it but it falls. There is a blinding flash. The ball spins like a silvery, green fireworks 'Catherine Wheel' and there is the sound of shattering glass. Max and Carla jump back in horror. Champ and Curly howl.

Chapter 2

"I'm sorry," gasps Carla. "I'm sorry," she whispers.

Grandpa pulls Nanna out of the way. Holly stands paralysed as

the remains of the ball disintegrate. Immediately they are

enveloped in the green, silvery mist, frozen in time, too stunned to

move. They feel the mist swirl around them. It has an intense

emotion about it, as if it is cross with them. They move closer

together and hold hands. Eventually, the mist softens and

becomes gentle again. It draws back into…

…the ball. They stare in absolute amazement. The ball is still

there. Even Nanna is totally bewildered. How can this be? They

all heard the sound of it breaking.

Grandpa is the first to move. He moves and kneels next to the

ball. They watch with bated breath as he reaches for it and picks it up. There is no reaction from it, no sound, no fireworks. The silvery, green mist swirls gently inside it. He lets out his breath.

"Let's get it inside."

Nanna finds her key and opens the door. They hurry in. Holly is last.

"Where do think we'll put it Em?"

"What about on the leadlight cabinet in the entrance," she suggests.

Grandpa leads them through the house to the alcove at the front door.

"Won't it roll off? asks Max, as Grandpa sets it down.

The base of the ball flattens. Grandpa lifts it up. It resumes its shape. He sits it down and again the base flattens.

"Wow! Impressive." Max is astounded.

"It looks quite at home," laughs Grandpa.

"Perhaps it is." Nanna smiles. "It seems to have a warm glow about it."

They look more closely. Nanna's right. The ball is shining with a soft pink light.

Holly moves, like a shadow, behind Nanna. Nanna takes her hand.

"Touch it," she entreats. "Go on. It won't hurt you."

"Go on Holly," plead Max and Carla.

Grandpa gives Holly a large encouraging smile. She takes a deep breath and reaches out. The soft pink light caresses her fingers. She lightly touches the ball with one finger. It changes from silvery green to a sparkling pink, white and violet. She hesitates.

"Keep going," whispers Nanna.

She touches with all her fingers. A gold ribbon of light flows through the ball, creating a pathway and revealing a small, closed book, its cover a shimmer of vibrant pink, violet and white light. Holly draws back. The golden pathway fades but the book remains in position. It emits a soft golden glow.

Nanna reaches out and touches the ball. She thinks she feels a light vibration. She indicates to Holly to touch it too. The vibration intensifies and the book seems to tremble.

"Can we open up the ball?"

Max's voice is whisper soft.

"No." Holly is definite. She removes her hand.

"Why not?" asks Carla. Holly doesn't answer.

"I don't think so," replies Nanna. She carefully lifts the ball and turns it over in her hands. Again it resumes its perfect shape. There appears to be no way of opening it. She gently places it back on the cabinet. It settles into position, the glowing book suspended in the centre.

They stand in silence, watching, waiting, wondering.

"It's stupid," declares Carla. "What good is a book if we can't read it? I'm going to have breakfast."

She moves towards the stairs but hesitates, torn between going and perhaps missing out on something more.

"Try touching it again, Holly," says Grandpa.

Holly touches it again. The book glows brighter.

"There's got to be a way," mutters Max. "Why don't we just ask it?"

"Oh brilliant," mocks Holly. "Why don't we just ask it?"

"That's an interesting idea, Max," grins Nanna.

Holly stares at her in disbelief.

"Give it a try."

"Um, er, well." Max fumbles for the right words. Carla chips in. She theatrically projects her voice and waves her arms about her.

"Oh, great ball. Tell us how to open the book!"

They all laugh, their attention on her. Suddenly, Max gasps. They immediately follow his gaze.

Inside the ball, the book trembles. The cover slowly opens and a page flutters and turns. On it, in an ancient script, are the words, *"Ask and you shall receive."*

Again, like a frozen tableau, they stand mesmerised. Time stands still. They cannot breathe. Then, without warning, the book gently closes and fades into the soft, silver, green mist, as if it had never been. The silence is intense. Nanna breaks it.

"Breakfast I think," she declares. "Come on, she urges, as they hesitate. "That's more than enough drama for one morning. We need food for thought".

"And time to digest," quips Grandpa with a smile. He tickles Max and Carla and chases them upstairs after Nanna. Holly follows more slowly, her mind a tangle of thoughts. She has one last look at the ball. Its golden glow brightens with a touch of pink. The mist momentarily clears to give her a brief glimpse of the book. She hurries upstairs to join the others.

Nanna and Grandpa have the usual array of cereals, mueslis and breads set up on the kitchen bench. Grandpa offers toast, eggs and bacon. Nanna makes the teas. She remembers Holly's i-Pod.

"Who has Holly's i-Pod?"

"Here, Nanna."

Carla pulls it out of her pocket. She starts to access the photos they took on the beach.

"Finish your breakfast first," advises Grandpa, as Max, toast in hand, leaps out of his chair.

"Watch your cup of tea! You'll have it all over the floor."

Grandpa grabs Max's cup just in time. He pulls Max back to his chair.

"The photos aren't going anywhere."

Nanna is thoughtful.

"Hmm. I think it might be a good idea if we copied them onto the computer."

"Why?" asks her husband.

"Just a feeling," she replies. I'll do it after breakfast.

"Finished!" Max stuffs the last of his toast in his mouth.

"That's gross," says Carla, doing the same.

"Can we look now?" she mumbles through her toast. Before Grandpa can answer, she has the i-Pod photos on screen. Max squeezes next to her.

"Wow! It's just as amazing as on the beach," he exclaims.

Grandpa and Nanna crowd behind them and watch in awe as Carla scrolls through the photos.

"It's like some Sci-Fi Fantasy Film," she declares. "With us in it and ......"

She turns to Holly, who is still seated at the table, her breakfast half eaten.

".... and you're the star," she adds.

Carla continues to scroll through the photos. The conversation is alive with speculation, rationalisation, possibility and impossibility.

The colour drains from Holly's face. A multitude of thoughts rush through her mind, most of them to do with everyone, including the ball, disappearing.

Suddenly there is silence. Holly looks up, startled. Did she speak out loud?

Nanna hears it first, then Holly. They turn towards the door to the upstairs landing.

Outside, Champ and Curly, briefly whine.

"What is it? asks Grandpa.

"Listen," whispers Nanna. "The hum from the beach. It's the ball."

"Yes!" Max and Carla hear it. The hum increases in volume and Grandpa, who is a little deaf, can hear it. As one, they move towards the stairs. Holly hangs back but the pull of the sound is too strong. As they gather, at the top of the stairs, the sound weaves through them, like a musical piece with silent words. Nanna tunes into the sound. She can almost pick out a word.

"Orb".

"It's an orb," she shares.

Her husband raises his eyebrows but says nothing. He is used to his wife's unusual perceptions.

They all listen intently, trying to hear what Nanna hears. The sound is gentle and soothing, washing over them like a wave. Then Nanna and Holly again hear the soft call.

"Hollllleeeee."

Holly gives a small gasp. Before she can say anything Max and Carla have scrambled down the stairs. Grandpa quickly follows them.

"Em, Holly," he calls. "Come. Come and look. It's brilliant!"

Nanna takes Holly's hand and they slowly walk down the stairs. There is a bright glow in the alcove. Grandpa and Max stand fixated in front of the cabinet. Carla is taking photos. Nanna and Holly move next to them. The ball, or orb, as it has told them, is perfectly clear, mist free. A halo of golden light illuminates the book inside. Once more the book is open. They move closer. Like before, there is a single sentence, in an ancient script.

It reads,

"Be careful what you ask for."

Blood rushes to Holly's head. The page flutters and turns.

Written on the new page are the words,

'Thoughts are very powerful.'

Nanna turns to Holly, with a gentle smile.

"What were you thinking up there?"

Holly half laughs and sheepishly admits that she was wishing that everyone, including the ball would disappear.

"Oh nice," says Carla. She takes another photo.

"It's okay for you," retorts Holly. "It's not your name it's calling. It's mine. You were going on and on about it all. I just want it to all go away."

"It sure ain't going away," drawls Max. He has a sudden thought. His face lights up.

"If it means what it says and it answered you, well… sort of answered, what you were thinking, does that mean if I wish for something I will get it?"

"Who knows," says Nanna. She grins. "Remember what it said."

"Yeh. Yeh. Be careful what you …".

He stops as another page turns. Grandpa reads the message.

"It is the intention that counts".

Max frowns.

"Uh? What's that supposed to mean?"

"I think it's about the purpose, the reason you want something," says Nanna.

"Is it for nice things or nasty things?"

We know what things you'd want," adds Holly sharply. "Nasty things".

Max glares at her.

"It's turning again".

Carla brings their attention back to the book as it slowly reveals the next page. They wait expectantly as the page settles.

"Life is like a returning boomerang."

Carla laughs loudly.

"It sounds like you Nanna. You're always saying things like that, like 'Life is a mirror'. Did you plant it on the beach?

"Nanna?" Max looks crestfallen.

Nanna grabs him in a bear hug.

"Do you really think I could do all those things? She laughs. "I know I have magic hands but the mist, the mounds of sand, the splintering glass, the book in the orb, the turning pages…"
She swings him around.

"Impossible, Max. This is incredible magic, something out of this world."

"So what do you think it's all about then," asks Grandpa. "Why us? Why Holly?"
Nanna lifts her hands and shrugs.

"I guess we'll just have to wait and see."

They all return their attention to the orb. The book trembles and then closes. Its shimmering cover of pink, violet and white relaxes.

"What a strange title," exclaims Carla.

For the first time they can see the Title on the cover. It's just called, *'A book'.*

Carla takes a photo. Nanna nods in approval and holds out her hand for the i-Pod. Carla passes it to her.

"Thanks Carla. I'll copy the photos onto my computer." She moves off to her office.

Grandpa and the children hang around for a while. Max tries some silly requests but the book remains still.

At last Grandpa suggests they'd better get moving because their parents are coming for lunch and the place needs to be tidied, beds made, dishes done and bodies washed.

"I can't wait to show mum and dad". Max punches the air with his fist. He punches Carla on the arm.

"Ow! That hurt."

She punches him back. They start to wrestle, knocking the cabinet and shaking the orb.

"Watch out, you idiots," yells Holly. "You'll break it ….. again".

Max and Carla ignore her.

She grabs the cabinet to steady it.

"Stop it you two," orders Grandpa. He pulls Carla away. She shrugs him off.

"I didn't start it," she grumbles.

"It doesn't matter who started it. I said stop it."

"Now look what you've done," shouts Holly.

"It's gone!"

There is stunned silence.

"It can't have just gone," Carla's mouth trembles.

She and Max start to search frantically for the orb.

"Well it has!" yells Holly. "It just came and now it's just gone and it's all your fault.

She storms off up the stairs.

"You didn't want it any way," Carla yells after her.

"You wanted it to disappear…." Her voice trails off. "…. and it has."

Grandpa hugs her as she bursts into tears. "It's not my fault," she sobs. "Is it?"

"No, of course not," he assures her.

"Perhaps it will come back," whispers Max.

"Let's wish for it to come back."

The three of them hold hands and silently wish for the orb to come back.

"And now, we'd better get moving," suggests Nanna, who has been watching from the door of her office. Disconsolate, Max and Carla hurry off. Nanna joins her husband in contemplating the empty space on the cabinet.

"What do you think," he says. She raises one eye brow in question.

"About the whole thing," he adds.

"It belongs there," she replies enigmatically. "It's for us all but mostly for Holly. She's the messenger."

Nanna gives her husband a big smile.

"Come on," she says, linking arms with him. "Amanda and Matthew will be here soon."

Grandpa eyes his wife suspiciously as they slowly make their way upstairs to their bedroom, to shower and dress and make their bed. There is silence in the rest of the house.

Chapter 3

There is no sign of the children when Nanna and Grandpa are finished. When they enter the large guest bedroom, an astonishing sight greets them. The beds are made and no clothes are in view. Grandpa opens a cupboard door. All the clothes are neatly hanging and the shoes are in place, in pairs. Nanna raises her eye brows in wonder.

"Wow!" breathes Grandpa as he follows her into the family room. "The model family," he whispers. Nanna suppresses a laugh.

Max and Carla are playing with the Lego and Holly is slumped in a chair, reading a book. They sheepishly grin as Nanna gives each of them a big hug and a kiss.

"More magic," she exclaims. "Thank you". She smiles mischievously at them. "Who knows what might happen next... if

I wish hard enough…" The children look sharply at her and half
stand.

"Just kidding," she laughs.

The sound of Champ and Curly barking, and rushing to the gate,
saves her from further scrutiny.

"It must be your mum and dad," declares Grandpa.

Carla and Max leap from their places and rush to the front door.

Holly slowly follows, with her grandparents. She laughs and asks
them.

"How long before Max gives them the whole story?"

"And how long before your dad reckons it's a load of nonsense?
responds Nanna with a big smirk.

"About now," laughs Grandpa, as his son-law, with Max dodging
and twisting his dad's pokes and tickles, struggles in the front
door. Max's words tumble out of his mouth as he desperately tries
to tell the story. Matthew greets them with a mocking grin. Nanna
welcomes him with a hug and kiss. He turns towards his father-in-
law

"Hi Henry. I see you haven't got them under control yet?"

"Yep, much the same as usual, Matt.," Grandpa shakes his hand and then turns, with a wide smile, to greet his daughter who is endeavouring to escape Curly's paws.

"Hi Mandi." She returns his smile. "Hi Dad. Hi Mum." She embraces them both. "Lots happening?"

"Mmmmmmmmmmm. You could say that," replies her mother. "We'll tell you about it after you've told us how the renovations are going."

"I don't think Max can wait that long," murmurs Holly, indicating with her head as Max continues to bombard his father. Carla joins Max in trying to convince their father that it's all true.

"Okay. Okay. I give in. Show me this ball or orb or what ever you call it".

Max and Carla hesitate.

"Well... come on then," he demands.

"It's uh, kind of... er ... um... disappeared...," Max's voice trails off.

His father coughs back a laugh. He turns to his mother-in-law and winks.

"The same crap, as usual," he cracks. "The family's always heaping shit on me too. Holly winces but Nanna just smiles.

"It's true," defends Holly. "We all saw it.

"That's right." Carla joins in. She pushes her dad. "Ask Grandpa." Grandpa nods in agreement.

"It must be true then," declares her dad. He playfully pushes her back.

"Sarcasm," snaps Holly, crossly, "Is the lowest form of wit." Her father gives her a silly smile.

She exchanges looks with Carla and Max.

Suddenly Matthew is under attack from his three children. He fends them off and races outside. They follow in hot pursuit, the dogs at their heels.

"Welcome to the mad house," laughs Nanna. She ushers her daughter upstairs.

We've photos, you know. I've copied them from Holly's i-Pod onto my computer."

"Really?" Amanda hides her smile but her father catches it.

"Really," he affirms. "We'll get Holly to show you, when they get back. Come on, I'll make a cuppa and you can tell us how the renovations are coming along".

The children finally catch their dad halfway across the beach. They tackle him and bring him to the sand, demanding that he listen and believe them. They poke and tickle him and the dogs lick him until he laughs and gasps.

"Okay. Okay. I give in. Get these dogs off me."

"Tell us you believe us first." Holly is firm.

"Yes. Yes. I believe you. There is an orb and ...," he splutters with laughter. They attack him some more. "There is an orb and it rose up from the sand...." He half chokes on another laugh. They torment him with more tickles. He puts on a serious face and tries again. "There is an orb and it rose up from the sand and called Holly's name."

"Go on," they threaten.

He continues. "When you dropped it, it smashed into smithereens and then reformed. Um and then... Hang on. It has a book inside it and its pages turn to give you your wish or the answer to your questions. Is that right?"

"Hmm. It'll do, I suppose," says Holly.

Max and Carla help him up. He brushes himself down and pushes the dogs away with his foot.

"Oooh. What's the smell? What's that on your trousers?" asks Carla, screwing up her nose in disgust.

Max shrieks with laughter and points to his dad's trousers. "Poo," he snorts. "You've been lying in dog poo". His dad's good humour quickly evaporates. He kicks angrily at the dogs.

"Aren't you supposed to pick up their shit? He yells.

"We do," retorts Carla, indignantly.

"Actually," says Holly. "It's the wrong colour for our dogs".

Carla looks at Holly in disbelief and rolls her eyes. Their dad is not amused.

"That'd be right," he fumes. "Just my luck. Come on let's get back".

He strides off towards the track. They follow slowly, making sure the dogs stay with them. Max is still doubled over with laughter. Carla cautions him. "Don't let dad see you. He's mad enough now." Max laughs even more.

"Don't you get it." he gasps. "The poo…the shit.. Dad talked about the shit… ," his voice fades off as Holly and then Carla grasp what he's saying.

"Oh my God", they exclaim together.

"Do you think it's the … ?"

"It did say thoughts are very powerful," Max reminds them.

"And words,' adds Holly "are spoken thoughts.

"It wouldn't would it?" sniggers Carla. They crack up.

Above the cabinet, in the alcove near the front door, a tiny speck of light appears. It settles on the cabinet.

Chapter 4

The children discretely follow their dad back to the house.

They find him in the laundry hastily trying to clean his trousers.

Holly offers to help but he ungraciously rejects her offer.

"I can do it," he snaps.

They make a hasty retreat, still smothering their laughter.

"What's up?" asks their mum as soon as they appear.

"Up?" wide eyed, they feign ignorance.

"Yes... something's up. I can always tell."

Max can't contain himself any longer. He bursts into laughter.

Dad got dog poo on his trousers.

"And that's funny?"

"No. It's what he said before, when we chased him." Carla adds.

Their mother looks puzzled.

"The orb." Nanna makes the connection straight away.

"Yes. Dad said mum was always heaping shit on him. The orb says you get what you ask for." Holly explains.

"So dad got what he was thinking about," adds Max.

"You've lost me." Amanda looks at her parents for enlightenment.

Nanna turns to Holly. "Why don't you get your i-Pod?" she suggests. "I put it next to your bed."

To her mother's amazement Holly dashes off.

"What have you been feeding her? She laughs. She is distracted by the sound of her husband stomping up the stairs. She turns to greet him.

"Ah. A bit of bother, eh?"

He glowers at her. "Bloody dogs."

"Not ours," defends Carla hastily, as Grandpa looks concerned.

"They should all be shot."

"Dad!" Carla is horrified. "Be careful what you wish for." Her father shakes his head in incredulity.

"What has Nanna been feeding you?"

"Here, Nanna. The i-Pod. Sorry. I couldn't find it." Holly

interrupts. She glares at Max. "Somebody must have moved it."

"It wasn't me," he retorts. Carla looks away.

Nanna quickly intervenes. She suggests they go into the family

room. At the table, Matthew and Amanda gather around their

children, as Holly turns the i-Pod on. She opens the files and

scrolls down to the morning's photos. The first photo shows the

beach scene and them standing in a group looking at something

on the sand. Carla and Grandpa are holding the dogs. There's

nothing on the sand; no mounds, no orb. She hastily scrolls to the

next photo and then the next and the next... nothing, just them on

the beach. She looks frantically at Nanna who's looking

perplexed.

"They were there," she confirms. "I copied them onto my

machine."

"Let me look." Max grabs the i-Pod. Holly snatches it back. They

struggle together until Grandpa pulls Max away.

"Steady on, "murmurs Grandpa. "There has to be some

explanation."

"Or it's all a big con," counters his son-in-law.

"It's not a con!" shouts Max, whacking his father. "We saw it."

Amanda eases Max away. She turns to Carla, hiding behind them all. "You're very quiet Carla," she says. Holly looks up sharply as Carla's face reddens. "You," she shouts. "You've done something. You've lost it all. What did you do?"

Carla bursts into tears. "I only sent some photos to Sara, she sobs. "The photos were still there then."

"Well they're not there now," yells Holly crossly.

Nanna puts her arms around Carla. "It's okay. It's okay," she soothes. "Lucky I copied the photos onto my computer. We can look at them there. Come on Holly."

Holly grumpily pushes back her chair. "She should leave my things alone," she mutters. "I wish she…" She stops suddenly, as awareness hits her. Max and Carla stand aghast.

"You wish what? asks their mother. "Nothing. I wish nothing."

Nanna lets go her breath.

Her daughter and son-in-law look totally confused. She smiles ingenuously at them. "Let's go and look at my computer," she offers.

Max bounds ahead of them, down the stairs. Carla and his parents close behind. When he suddenly stops at the bottom they cannon into him. "For goodness sake Max," snaps his father. "It's back," breathes Max. "It's back!" He shouts. "Nanna, it's back!" He charges forward into the alcove. Holly and Carla eagerly push past their parents to join him.

Grandpa turns to Nanna and smiles. "Looks like our wish came true," he calls to Max and Carla. "Come on you two," he adds to Amanda and Matthew. "What are you waiting for? This is the moment of truth."

The three children impatiently wait for the adults to join them. Sure enough, as if it had never left, the orb, surrounded by a soft gold, pink light, is sitting on the small cabinet in the alcove. Inside the orb, the silvery green mist swirls in a delicate dance.

42

Their parents stare memorised by the spectacle. Matthew reaches out to touch it. "Dad! Careful," warns Max.

His father looks at him curiously. He moves closer.

"Dad!" hisses Max. Matthew instinctively draws back but not before the orb emits a small series of sparks. He steps back a pace.

Holly laughs. "It likes you dad, as much as it likes Max."

Amanda leans in closer to get a better view. "What is it mum?"

"We don't really know."

"Look," urges Carla. "It's clearing. You can see the path to the book..."

"Book?" Amanda looks confused.

"Don't worry Mandi, we'll explain later," whispers Grandpa.

As they watch, the mist clears along a gold ribbon of light, to reveal the small book, suspended in space. Its cover shimmers in pink, violet and white light.

"Do you think it has a message?" whispers Max.

"Just wait," counsels Nanna. "Be patient."

They wait expectantly. Matthew and Amanda exchange bewildered looks. The book trembles.

"Yessssssss," breathes Max excitedly. The cover turns to reveal a page with the ancient scripted words,

"Thoughts are very powerful."

"We've had that one," says Max disappointed.

"Perhaps you haven't got the message yet," suggests Holly. Max sticks his tongue out at her. Carla gives a snicker and Max kicks at her with his knee.

The orb emits sharp sparks of light. "I don't think it likes your bickering," cautions Nanna. They stop immediately. The orb settles and again they watch as a new page turns with another message, written in the same ancient script.

"You can hold a thought for a second before it crystallises into being; words, actions, feelings."

Holly gasps. "That's what you did upstairs," says her mother.

"You stopped your thought."

Holly nods. "It also said, *'Ask and you shall receive.'*", she explains. She turns to her father. "Do you believe us now? She asks.

"Yep. Nanna's really out done herself this time", he jokes.

The orb sends out a bolt of light in his direction. He jumps back and puts up his hands in surrender.

"Okay. Okay. I withdraw that comment," he hastily amends.

The book quickly changes to a new page. They all crane forward to read the words.

"Believe the unbelievable."

"Wow!" Amanda laughs. "I think that's for you Matt." Max and Holly wholeheartedly agree.

"Yeh, Dad." Matthew makes a face at them. Nanna smiles her amused smile and raises her eyebrows. She turns to Carla who has been very quiet. "What do you think, Carla?" she asks. Carla just shrugs and refocusses her attention on the orb.

It trembles and then seems to settle before it slowly closes. The soft golden light around it dims. The iridescent coloured lights on the cover become still. The session is over.

"Is there any more," asks Matthew.

 "Isn't that enough to start with?" laughs Nanna. "Perhaps you could look at the photos now and the children could tell you all about it, while Henry and I get lunch.

"Just give me a moment and I'll just get them up on the computer."

While Nanna turns on her computer, the children start recounting their early morning adventure.

"Here you are," says Nanna. They're all there." "Holly's in charge," she adds. "Lunch'll be in about half an hour."

Lunch is home made soup and crusty bread. There is only one topic of conversation, 'The Orb'. What is it? Where did it come from? Why did it choose them? Even Matthew is under its spell. He starts to expand on wonderful plans for making their fortune with it. Grandpa notices that Carla is not joining in nor eating her lunch.

"What's up?" he asks her. "Nothing,' she mutters in reply. "She's sulking," says Holly.

46

"Am not." Carla reddens.

"Yes you are," declares Holly. "Cos you lost the photos".

"I didn't, I…,"

Nanna gently interrupts.

"It doesn't matter," she smiles. "Come on eat your lunch."

"I don't like it," Carla mumbles.

"Of course you do," says Grandpa. "It's your favourite. Nanna made it especially for you."

"Well I don't like it today."

"You haven't even tried it," he says.

Matthew is suddenly tired of the whole thing. "Stop being silly. Just eat it," he orders.

"This not eating just because you're upset is stupid. Children are starving in Africa you know. They'd die for a meal like this. Besides, I thought bread was one of your …".

Amanda touches him on the arm to stop him. Everyone watches as Carla takes a mouthful of bread. She chews it slowly, her eyes on her plate. There is a sense of relief and the conversation returns to the topic of the orb.

Just as Matthew starts to expand on ideas as to how the orb could be used to make their fortune, Carla pushes back her chair and gets up from the table. She still hasn't eaten much lunch.

"That's stupid dad," she snaps.

"Where are you going?" he demands in reply.

"To the toilet. Is that all right?" She flounces off.

"Gone to spit out the bread, more likely," says Max. Holly glares at him. His father looks at him sharply. "Just joking," Max hastily adds.

Carla decides to use the downstairs toilet. As she passes the orb she senses a change in its appearance. She stops and moves closer to it. The book is closed. The colours on its cover seem to pulsate. They ebb and flow, moving in and out of the orb. Like a magnet, she is drawn towards it. She reaches out to touch it. The light moves suddenly towards her. She gives a small shriek as it grabs her and pulls her in. She is in a swirling tunnel of light. It is projecting her forward, forward into a strange parched landscape of large bare rocks, cracked soil and a blazing sun in a blue sky.

Terrified, she shrinks back against the rocks. She is on the outskirts of a small, mud built village. She smells the heat and the poverty. Several young, raggedly clad children are hanging around one of the huts, waiting. Carla wonders what they are waiting for. They're very thin, their rib bones prominent in their skin, their bellies distended. Several women and a couple of older children struggle pass her, carrying large baskets or containers on their heads. The young children rush to greet them, pulling at their skirts. The women and older children put down their containers. A girl, about Carla's age, enters one of the huts and returns with some bowls. She carefully lifts one of the containers and divvies up the supply of water. A few elderly men emerge from one of the huts to join them. The girl offers them the water first. One of the younger children accidentally knocks over one of the bowls, spilling the precious portion of water. He is quickly cuffed by one of the men. The girl shares her portion with the boy.

The women are mixing ingredients from one of their containers. They add a little of the water to make it into a paste. To Carla it looks like a few dry seeds, mixed with flour. The women carefully divide it between the expectant adults and children. When all is prepared, they sit in a circle and one of the women offers a prayer of thanks and a blessing for the food and water. Carla can feel their hunger. Her stomach hurts. She feels the excitement and pleasure that the anticipated meal brings, the relief, that for today, they have something to eat and drink. The waves of their emotion wash over her.

There is sudden excitement in the group. She is spotted. One of the women signals to her to come and join them. She shrinks further back into the rock. The men send the girl to get her, to share their meal. She feels faint and suddenly is pulled back into the swirling tunnel of light, moving back, back, back into the alcove at her grandparents' house. The floor trembles under her feet for a moment. Then all is as it was. The orb sits silently on Nanna's cabinet. She blinks and shakes her head. Did it happen? Or did she imagine it.

When she returns to the family room, it's as if no time has passed. The meal is half finished and her father is still waxing lyrical about plans for the orb.

"That was quick," Holly comments. Carla just smiles and sits down. The food in front of her looks and smells delicious. She savours each mouthful of soup and the texture and crunch of the bread. Nanna gives her a quizzical look but says nothing. The meal finishes with nanna's chocolate caramel slices and then fruit. Nothing has ever tasted so good. Her mother breaks her reverie. "So what do you think the orb is, Carla," she asks. Carla thinks for a moment. "We'll have to ask it," she says.

After lunch they say goodbye to their parents who as usual, have pressing work commitments, plus the renovations to attend to. The children need to stay at their grandparents for a little longer, at least until the end of the summer holidays.

"There's no kitchen at the moment," explains Amanda. "Dad and I are cooking on the camp stove, in the laundry and washing up in a basin".

"At least you have something nice to cook. Not like the starving people in Africa", says Carla unexpectedly." Her mother gives her a 'well, what's that all about' look.

The children promise to keep their parents informed about the orb and its messages. "And no doubt," adds Nanna with a lopsided grin, "Matthew will keep working on the commercial aspect of it all."

"Someone has to support the family," he replies.

As they return to the house, after farewelling the parents, they notice that the shimmering pink, violet and white light surrounding the orb appears to be brighter than before. They look more closely. A new page is open. Carla reads it.

"I am the light of the Universe."

Is the orb answering their mother's question?

Nanna tries another question.

"What is the light of the universe? "

They watch with bated breath but nothing changes.

After ten minutes they give up.

The afternoon passes with a spirited game of cricket, on the beach. Even Holly is motivated to leave her novel and join in. The dogs think it's fabulous. They are excellent outfielders, especially if the ball lands in the sea.

When they return, they check the orb but nothing has changed

After dinner they watch television.

Before they go to bed they check the orb but it's still the same.

Chapter 5

That night Holly dreams she is sailing in a glowing ball, through the stars, into the depths of the universe, towards a dazzling white light. She enters the light and momentarily is stunned by the brightness. Then she passes through it into nothingness. The soft darkness around her is like liquid velvet. The space is endless; the quietness and peace totally encompassing. She feels completely safe.

A single word resonates within her. 'Love.'

She drifts back into sleep.

Next morning, despite her apprehension, she is up before anyone else. She has to check the orb. With her heart in her mouth, she tiptoes down the stairs. A silvery pink mist rises to greet her.

A new page is open and on it a single word.

"*Love.*"

Goosebumps travel up her arms and legs. Her heart starts to race.

She turns to scurry back to her room......

...straight into Nanna's arms. She yelps out loud. She is shaking.

"Whoa. Easy", whispers Nanna, hugging Holly close to her.

"I dreamed it," gasps Holly. "I dreamed it."

Nanna studies the word on the open page. "Let's get a drink," she

suggests and steers Holly into the kitchen.

Wrapped in a blanket, Holly nervously sips her hot chocolate. She

tells Nanna all about her dream. It is still very vivid in her

memory. Nanna is thoughtful. She asks if Holly has ever had a

dream like that before. Holly shakes her head.

"It was so real," she says.

"And peaceful and beautiful?" suggests Nanna.

"Yes but it's so scary," replies Holly. Nanna asks why but Holly

can't explain.

"It just is."

"Where do you think you were?" asks Nanna.

Holly shrugs,

They are interrupted by the arrival of Grandpa who is surprised to see them, especially Holly, up before him. His wife explains what has happened. He gives Holly a reassuring hug and tells her that there are some things that just can't be explained. Though he has to admit that this is a little more unusual than anything he's ever encountered and he's been around for a fairly long time.

"Let's take the dogs out for an extra early walk", he suggests. Holly looks doubtful so Nanna recommends they go to the park instead of the beach.

The walk is completely uneventful and they return home to find Carla and Max monitoring the orb.

Even though they're surprised to see Holly up at such an early hour, the orb is a more powerful curiosity. They turn excitedly turn towards them.

"Nanna, it's got a new message!" exclaims Max. Carla nods

"It's a bit strange," he adds.

"The heart of the universe."

Nanna, Grandpa and Holly exchange glances. Max and Carla look from one to the other. Holly looks away.

"Well!" they both burst out together. "What does it mean?" demands Carla.

"Perhaps over breakfast", suggests Grandpa.

During breakfast they retell the story of Holly's dream and the orb's message but it doesn't really account for the latest message.

The heart of the universe.

Holly replays the events in her head and remembers Nanna's question.

"It's answering your question Nanna', she says. "You asked me 'Where do you think you were?'"

"It's saying I was in the heart of the universe".

"Wow! That's awesome", exclaims Max. The others contemplate the information in silence; what was it all about, why them, who was it? A million questions race around their heads. Had they found the orb or had it found them?

Holly suddenly sits bolt upright. "It's turning", she says. "The pages are turning".

No one queries her. As one they race out of the dining room and down to the alcove.

The page is still trembling.

Holly read the words.

"I am the words of the universe. You are the voice."

The book closes. This is even more perplexing. Are there more words? How could they be the voice? Who is the voice?

They wait but the book remains closed.

All day it remains closed and the next and the next.

Chapter 6

On the third day, when they wake, it's raining. The sea is dark and stormy. Black clouds hang on the horizon and a strong wind buffets the house. Despite the weather they take their morning walk. The full force of the wind hits them as soon as they enter the beach. They stagger across the sand, shielding their face from wind and grit. When the clouds suddenly burst even Grandpa admits it's a no go and they'd better get home fast.

Max and Carla race ahead, eager to get first showers. Holly grumbles as she trudges behind Nanna and Grandpa and the dogs. By the time she gets back she's soaked. Rain water trickles down her neck inside her clothes, down her legs and into her shoes. She glares at the orb as she passes it. Does she imagine that it's laughing at her discomfort? She steps back to check. The book is still closed but there's a slight pulsing in the light. "Well?" she snaps. There's no response. She storms off. "Stupid thing," she mutters.

After breakfast Grandpa sets up the table tennis. Nanna coaxes Holly to leave her books and join them in a Round Robin competition. Competition is fierce. Max is determined to win, smashing the ball at every chance. Even Holly wins a game against Grandpa. Finally it's just Nanna and Max. The more points Nanna wins the more aggressive and erratic Max becomes. Nanna remains calm and focussed. Holly and Carla cheer her on and Grandpa applauds them both. At twenty/ twenty-one, Max serves to save the match. He studies Nanna poised at the other end of the table. He hates to lose, especially to Nanna who's really pretty old. He angrily serves the ball down the centre, straight at her. It misses by a mile. The girls and Grandpa clap and cheer. "Nanna's the table tennis champ," they chant. "Great game," exclaims Grandpa.

Max starts to throw his bat at the table but catches Nanna's eye.

She smiles, raises her eyebrows and gives a slight shake of her

head. He stops and grudgingly congratulates her. They shake

hands.

"Well done," she says. "You know you're a much better player

than I am. The difference is that I'm like the eye of the storm,

calm and in control of my power. You're like the edges of the

storm, running wild, filled with power but out of control."

"The orb has spoken," laughs Grandpa. The children exchange

glances. As one they race to the alcove to look at the orb. Nothing

seems to have changed. The book is closed yet something feels

different.

"It's like it's waiting", whispers Carla.

"Yes," agrees Holly. "But for what".

"Maybe for lunch," suggests Nanna as she heads for the kitchen.

After lunch, as there's no let up in the weather, Nanna and

Grandpa give them permission to use their i-pads to connect with

their friends and social networks and to play games.

"No War Games, Max," warns Grandpa.

Late in the afternoon, Carla is bored. Her friends are busy and Holly is reading. Nanna is helping Grandpa in the garage. She finds Max in his bedroom. As usual, despite not being allowed to, he's playing War Games. Carla stands for a moment, watching. He's so focussed on his game. His face is tense as he fires shot after shot at the soldiers on the screen. He suddenly notices her and irritably waves her away. Undeterred Carla leans forward and presses a key to fire at a sniper. She misses and Max loses some men and points. Irate, he shoves her away. The interruption and distraction, gets him 'shot' and he loses the game. He lashes out, just missing her. She laughs and dodges away.

"It's just a game," she says. "You couldn't be a real soldier," she taunts him. "You're too wimpy." Max loses his temper and charges after her, catching her at the door to her room. He grabs her and thumps her on the back.

Carla shrieks. "That hurt," she gasps. She breaks free and escapes into her room, slamming the door against him. Max hears her muttering and threatening all manner of things, revenge and retaliation. He rudely gestures after her and stomps back to his room. He reloads his game.

As he watches the Game slowly reform he experiences the strangest sensation, an incredible intense vibration in his hands and a ringing in his ears. He feels as if he's being called. "Maaaaaxxx. Maaaaaxxx.". It reverberates in his head. He presses his hands against his head. "Maaaaaxxx.". He knows it's the orb calling him. He doesn't know how but suddenly he's there beside it.

Max senses a change in its appearance. He moves next to it. The book is closed. The colours on its cover seem to pulsate. They ebb and flow, moving in and out of the orb. Like a magnet, he is drawn towards it. He reaches out to touch it. The light turns red and moves suddenly towards him. He gives a small shriek as it grabs him and pulls him in. He is in a swirling tunnel of light. It is projecting him forward, forward into a strange parched landscape of unfamiliar partly demolished buildings, rubble strewn streets and a blazing sun in a blue sky.

Men, women and children are fleeing, desperately seeking shelter. He is surrounded by the sound of guns and grenades. Jet fighters are overhead. He watches as a bomb falls and explodes just metres away from him. He hears the anguished cries of the wounded. He smells the heat and the sickening stench of burning flesh. He is in the middle of a war. All around him people struggle to support each other and escape. Sickened, he feels the nausea rise in his throat. He staggers and is almost caught up in the surge of those fleeing when he notices a group of fighters moving towards him.

At that moment, he realises he's holding a gun. It feels cold and heavy in his hands. He instinctively edges closer to the nearest building and raises the gun to his shoulder. He focusses. One of the fighters is in his sight. Max can see him clearly.

"Shoot!" screams a voice in his head but he can't. He is paralysed. He can't pull the trigger.

He is spotted.

As Max throws himself to the ground, one of the combat fighters levels his gun and fires. Max feels a sharp pain in his left shoulder. The bullet's impact lifts him and tosses him against the building. His head strikes the wall. Blood spurts from his shoulder. Stars explode in his head as the pain surges through his body. Then there is darkness.

"Max! Max!" Carla's concerned voice breaks through his unconscious mind. "Max! Are you okay?"

He is slumped against the wall of the alcove. Carla grabs his shoulder and he gasps in agony. She jumps back.

"What's wrong? You look like you've seen a ghost"

"I've been....." Max's voice trails off as he inspects his shoulder. There's nothing there. No blood, no gaping hole, no gunshot wound at all. Only the pain.

"You've been ....?" Carla's eyes widen. She stares at Max. Max stares back. In the silence they both understand.

"What're you two up to?" Holly's voice breaks the silence. She looks from one to the other. They stare back.

Instinctively, she turns to look at the orb. She lets out a long slow breath. Carla and Max follow her gaze. The orb is encased in a soft green mist. As the mist clears along the gold ribbon of light, the book slowly opens.

The three children move in closer, mesmerised by the turning pages.

"What's happening?" asks Nanna who has silently joined them.

"Max? Holly? Carla?"

They jump like startled rabbits. Max wonders how long Nanna has been there.

Carla recovers first. She looks at the orb. The pages have settled. She reads them out loud.

"Love conquers all."

"As opposed to hate, violence…..and war?" Nanna raises an eyebrow at Max. He turns scarlet. Carla nods very slowly, several times. Embarrassed, Max pokes her in the arm and mumbles something indecipherable. Holly stares intently at the orb. The soft green light seems to pulsate around it. The hairs on the back of her neck stand on end. Her eyes widen with sudden awareness.

"What did it do Max?" she demands. She grabs him and shakes

him. He clutches his shoulder in pain. Nanna holds her back.

Holly turns to Carla. "Carla?"

Max tries to speak but Carla finds her voice first.

"It zapped me and pulled me into it!

Holly turns pale and shakes her head in disbelief.

"It did!" Carla adds heatedly, almost in tears. Nanna puts her arm

around her.

"Me too! declares Max.

"We believe you. We believe you," Nanna assures him. "It's fine.

Everything's fine." She contemplates the orb. Its light gently

pulsates and changes from green to pink to violet. The pages of

the book are at rest. She detects a deep hum and realises from the

look on Holly's face that she hears it too.

Holly opens her mouth to speak.

"It's stopped raining!" declares Grandpa coming in with two over

excited dogs.

"Who's coming for a walk?" He suddenly becomes aware of the disquiet of the tension. "Is everything okay?" he asks.

"Yes!" declares Max. He frowns at his sisters as they start to disagree. "It's all okay. A walk sounds great!"

Grandpa raises his eyebrows at Nanna.

"Later," she promises. "a walk and then afternoon tea. Isn't that right?" she asks the three children.

They wholeheartedly agree. Max and Carla race Grandpa and the dogs out of the door. Nanna gives Holly a quick hug and takes her hand. Holly is very quiet on the way to the beach. Nanna assures her that it'll be all right. Holly isn't so sure. Why is the orb talking to her? What does it want? She just wants to go back to the fantasy in her books. Why her?

"It's chosen you because you're special, Holly."

Holly jumps. Can Nanna read her thoughts? Suddenly all her concerns disappear, like cobwebs being blown away. It's as if a heavy weight has been lifted from her shoulders.

"It could have asked me!" She laughs at the ridiculousness of her comment. "Race you to the beach, Nanna!" She sprints off leaving her grandmother far behind.

The beach is beautiful, fresh and shiny. The wind has eased and the water has settled into tiny white caps. A shaft of sunlight breaks through the clouds and creates a path of light across the water. Holly joins Carla, Max and the dogs in a mad romp along the beach to the dunes at the far end. They release their pent up energy and tension by racing up and down the dunes. Nanna leisurely follows, catching up with her husband at the water's edge. They stand together, arms linked, and laugh at the antics of the children and dogs. For a moment the orb is forgotten.

Over afternoon tea, the three children share their experiences. They discuss the similarities and differences. Nanna finds a note book and carefully records their experiences and the words so far revealed in the pages of the book. They share their ideas and thoughts. Everyone agrees that Holly seems to be the chosen one but no one can offer a sensible explanation as to why.

"Perhaps", suggests Carla. "It thought you'd be the most accepting, seeing you've always got your head stuck in a weird Sci Fi sort of book."

Holly glares at her. "Better than your lolly dolly love ones", she retorts.

"If looks could kill", replies Carla.

"Don't mention killing, please", begs Max, ruefully rubbing his shoulder. "I hope that we find out soon why the orb's here and what it wants."

Then, as one, they all hear it, that deep hum, vibrating through the soles of their feet and ringing in their ears. It's the orb. Holly jumps up quickly and races down to the alcove, the others in hot pursuit.

"A new page," breathes Holly." They crowd around the orb. Holly reads the message.

"Go with the flow."

In a flick of an eyelid, Holly has a vivid image of a small stream, at its source, high in the mountains, tumbling downhill over small rocks, gathering speed and strength as it travels and becomes a river. She sees it become a torrent as it races through a narrow gorge, cascading over large boulders, before dropping, as a spectacular waterfall into a deep pool, metres below. It gradually slows until it enters a magnificent lake, surrounded by tall leafy trees. Fish and bird life abounds. The stillness of the lake perfectly reflects the blue sky and surrounding vegetation. She feels the absolute peace. Then it is gone, as the wind whips up the waters of the lake, as it continues its journey and enters a new river system. She follows it, as it passes through farm land and then many towns, eventually becoming sluggish and stagnant, filled with rubbish and pollution. She sighs. The vision clears and reforms and she sees the river refreshed, its water clear and healthy, as it hurries to the sea. She smiles and instantly becomes aware of where she is. She blinks and refocuses. Everyone does the same.

"Well, that's pretty clear," declares Grandpa.

The others all agree and Holly wonders how they pictured "Go with the flow".

Chapter 7

For the next couple of days nothing unusual happens.
Well almost ….. The orb continues to glow in varying shades of
pink and green and each morning the mist clears along a gold
ribbon of light, to reveal the small book, suspended in space and a
page turns to reveal a new message for them.

It becomes a daily ritual to gather in the alcove and read the
messages. They try to interpret them but it's not always easy.

"Observe the nature of Nature.

Be in two minds or three.

Look in the spaces between the words."

"They don't make sense," declares Max one morning. "Why
doesn't it speak in plain English?"

The orb brightens and a page quickly turns. They all read the
words.

"Words are limiting."

Holly has a moment of insight. "It uses metaphors."

"Of course," exclaims Nanna, tapping her head with her fingers. "I should have known that. It's speaking to our unconscious mind which likes images, patterns, stories, emotions, feelings and the imagination rather than the logical word-structured nature of our conscious minds. I use it in hypnosis."

"That doesn't make the messages any clearer or easy to understand," replies Carla.

"Not for our conscious mind," agrees Nanna, "but our unconscious mind understands."

Grandpa frowns. "So are you suggesting, Em, that we don't try to interpret the messages? His wife nods.

"We just, 'Go with the flow,'" drawls Carla.

"Like in my kayak," says Grandpa with a smile.

"In your Kayak!" teases Nanna with a laugh.

Grandpa gives her a mock offended look and then raises his eyebrows in a question.

"Like doing Tai Chi," adds Nanna.

"Like at the end of a footy match at the MCG."

Carla ignores Max's look of amusement.

"Like the journey of a river," supplies Holly.

There's silence as they wait for Max.

"Well......and? Grandpa asks.

"And like on my skateboard," Max finishes. "I get it!" He pumps
his hand in the air. "I get it".

They all laugh.

The orb's glow ebbs and flows, out and in, brighter and paler, as a
new page turns. It's almost as if it's laughing with them.

"You see what you want to see."

Life switches into real holiday mode. Nanna and Grandpa take the
children Tree Surfing. There are ropes and pulleys, suspension
bridges, steps and obstacles set up high in the trees ending in a
very long flying fox. Some of the challenges are quite difficult
and scary but even Holly, who's not known for her athleticism,
successfully tackles them.

It seems to Nanna that there's a greater tolerance, patience, co-
operation and understanding between the children. They work

better together as a team rather than in competition, giving each other support and encouragement. There's less bickering and more laughing. They have a greater awareness of their surroundings and what's going on about them and best of all; they spend less time on their electric devices and more time at the beach and in the garden. Of course they're not perfect and there are some mini eruptions but generally things are flowing smoothly. Even the dogs appear less frenetic on their beach walks.

This feeling continues when they take the children home to see how the renovations are progressing. The house is in semi chaos but their dad assures them that there is progress. The kitchen is almost in place and they can cook. Before lunch, they take a tour of the house. The bathrooms and bedrooms are gutted so it will obviously be some time before the children can return. Their parents are hopeful it'll be ready by the time school resumes. The children hope it won't. Life at Nanna's and Grandpa's has suddenly become very interesting.

During lunch, the children bring their parents up-to-date with all latest activities of the orb. Amanda shakes her head in wonder. She watches and listens in amazement as her three children, backed by her father, describe in vivid detail, their experiences with the orb.

Even though their father jokes and teases them, his scepticism has gone. As he starts to outline his wonderful plans for promoting the orb, Amanda leans across to her mother. She has noticed the difference in the children's behaviour and attitudes.

"Don't know what you've been feeding them," she whispers. "But keep it up."

Her mother smiles and lifts her hands. "Not me," she whispers back. "All credit to the orb."

"Really?" Amanda is thoughtful. "We obviously need to increase its influence," she murmurs. "There are others who'd benefit." She points at her husband who is becoming quite animated, inspired by his entrepreneurial plans for the orb.

"You're so right," laughs her mother. "And not just our ...." She pauses as a familiar hum resonates in her ears. The others hear it too.

"Dad. Dad!" Holly reaches across the table to tap her father.

"It's the orb." Her father carries on oblivious, as the hum becomes louder.

"DAD!" the three children shout in unison.

Suddenly sparks strike the table in front of their father. He sits back flabbergasted.

The family holds their breath, waiting for his reaction.

"Holy Moly! Whew! What was that?" He looks around and then under the table.

"I don't think the orb likes your ideas, Matt." Grandpa pats his son-in-law on the back.

Matthew laughs. "I think I'll stick to renovations and cooking." He leaves the table to serve up the desserts.

"Perhaps it's already working its magic," Amanda whispers to her mother. "Have the children tried the Social Networks, on the web?" she asks, returning to their former topic. Nanna nods her head. Her daughter listens while the three children explain how all the photos and most of their messages just disappear. Their friends receive only bits and pieces; a word here and there. Nanna explains that she still has the original photos on her computer. "We'll have to be patient. I'm sure something will happen to spark it."

Matt returns with dessert and the conversation briefly turns to the renovations, friends and work before returning to more speculations about the purpose of the orb. Matthew is showing signs of impatience, eager to get back to work.

"Keep us informed." Amanda pushes back her chair, ready to clear the table. She is delightfully surprised by the immediate helpful response from her children and exchanges bemused looks with her husband. The table is quickly cleared and the dishes washed and put away.

"Perhaps miracles do happen," murmurs Matthew to his mother-in law as he and Amanda farewell them. She smiles and gives him a gentle punch on the arm.

"The best is yet to come," she says. "We'll keep you informed."

As the car drives off, Amanda calls out to her mother. "Let's try word of mouth!"

Nanna give her the thumbs up.

"Oh sure mum," drawls, Holly dryly. "We'll simply drop it in somewhere in the conversation.... Oh, by the way, have we mentioned our orb...it just happened to rise up out of the sand..."

The following week is filled with activities. The weather is idyllic, blue skies, little wind and thirty degree days. Most of the time is spent at the beach. The children are all excellent swimmers. Except in a very low tide, the water is quite deep close to the beach. A small reef of sand, rock, sea grasses and kelps separates the inner channel from the outer channel. The sea is a brilliant aqua inside the reef and a deep ultramarine beyond it. It sparkles in the sunlight. Gentle low, rolling waves break in white foam along the edges. The reef is about one hundred and fifty metres from the shore. At low tide they can stand on the reef. They paddle out in Grandpa's kayak to dive and snorkel in the deeper outer channel. Grandpa and the two dogs swim out to join them. The water is so clear they can see the details of the small sea horses and fishes hiding in the grasses and kelps.

On the Friday there is even a pod of dolphins close to the reef. Nanna keeps the dogs on the beach and the dolphins swim close to where the children and Grandpa are standing on the reef. They allow Max, with his underwater camera, to take photos of them leaping out of the water and then doing dives and back flips. It's as if they are putting on a show especially for them. The more the children applaud, the more the dolphins perform. From the shore it looks to Nanna as if they are wrapped in a light green sea mist. At last as the tide turns to come in, the dolphins give a farewell salute and the pod heads out to sea. Grandpa and the girls swim back to shore, while Max paddles the kayak.

"How cool was that Nanna!" Max is over the moon. Even before the kayak has beached, he leaps from it, camera in hand. "I've got the best pictures; just the best pictures. Look!" He drops onto the sand next to her, spraying sand all over her and the dogs. The dogs escape into the water to join Grandpa. Nanna shakes off the sand and spreads a towel for the girls who are securing the kayak. Grandpa puts up the beach umbrella to cast shade so they can see the photos.

"Wow!" Nanna is impressed. Max has taken a video. They all gather close to watch it. The clarity and detail are extraordinary. Max soaks up their praise.

As it's the summer holidays and a long weekend, the beach is quite busy. Several families who are camping in the foreshore caravan park, further down the beach, and some neighbours join them for a game of cricket. They choose sides, campers versus the locals. The competition is fierce. When the ball is lost at sea, they laughingly call it a draw. One of the camping families invites them to the caravan park for a barbecue dinner.

The night is still and balmy. The sun is just below the treetops when they arrive with their hamper of salads and meats. The campers make them welcome. Max and Carla disappear with several children to the playground nearby.

Holly feels more at home with the adults. They gather around the barbecues. Conversation is easy but talking about the orb never seems to fit in. The smell of frying onions, sausages and meats drifting through the camping ground draws a large crowd. They sit at large wooden bench tables, laden with food and drinks. Grandpa thinks it's a perfect finish to a perfect day. Conversation dwindles to a soft murmur.

As the evening draws in, Holly moves to sit on a swing in the playground. She invites some of the younger children to join her for a story. They sit in a circle around her. The unusual sight attracts more children and some parents. Holly starts her story. "Once upon a time…." The audience listens, spellbound, as she weaves a magical story about a beautiful orb, found on this very beach. She describes the orb and its discovery in detail. They follow her every word as she reveals some of its secrets. Max,

Carla, Nanna and Grandpa watch from the sidelines. They too are mesmerised by her voice.

It's almost dark, the last rays of the sun forming a golden path across the sea, and the first stars are appearing, as she finishes and she realises that not only the children but the adults too are captured by her tale. There is a disappointed sigh when she stops.

"What happens next?" asks one of the children.

Holly touches her finger to her mouth and in a hushed voice replies. "You have to come back tomorrow night. It's nearly bed time now."

The children beg for more but Holly is firm. She promises to come back the next evening. The audience reluctantly starts to disperse. They all make their farewells and take their leave, heading back along the beach to their track. Even when the caravan park lights have disappeared, they can hear excited murmurs of the children and their parents.

"Well done Holly," says Grandpa wrapping his arm about her shoulders, as they make their way through the bush back to the house. "I felt like I was watching a movie."

"That was so cool," declares Max.

"Awesome," agrees Carla.

"Just brilliant," adds Nanna. The dogs bark their approval.

Holly feels a warm rosy glow flow through her. It was easy. She saw it all in her mind's eye; like a movie as Grandpa said. She just told the truth.

When they enter the house the glow around the orb is warm and rosy. A new page is open. Nanna reads it for them.

"Trust that the time is right."

Nanna gives Holly a big hug. It seems the time is right.

They discuss the events of the day and then watch television for a while before going to bed.

Tomorrow they are having lunch with Nanna's and Grandpa's close friends Laura and John Parry and their grandchildren

Louella and Ben. The five children have known each other forever. Their parents are great friends.

Despite the fact that with age, Laura and John have become gloomy and negative about many aspects of their life and have developed different interests, the two families have remained very good friends. John is very cynical about Nanna's hypnosis, meditation and Reiki and can't resist presenting arguments against all matters related to them. He certainly won't believe in an orb that has a mysterious book embedded in it and offers advice about how to improve their lives. He'll need proof. Laura will waver between wanting to believe and not believing. Holly is sure she can convince Louella and Ben.

The morning is overcast and the beach deserted when they go for their early morning walk. The euphoria of the previous evening is replaced by a slightly gloomy feeling. Even the dogs are lethargic. As they walk, they discuss whether or not to talk about the orb with Laura and John. Grandpa is doubtful but the children say why not. Holly suggests if they need proof that Nanna could print a couple of their orb photos and they can take them with them.

Once this is decided their mood immediately lightens.

After breakfast, Nanna opens her computer and loads the photos.

They look like something out of a Sci Fi movie. She prints two,

one from the beach and one showing the book with the words

'believe the unbelievable'. She studies them carefully. ". The

prints are sharp and clear in every detail

"Wow!" says Max, coming up behind her. "Great photos!"

"Yes," she replies. "But I don't recall us taking any photos except

on that first morning. This message came later"

"Perhaps Carla or Holly took them,' suggests Max. "Or

Grandpa," he adds cheekily as Grandpa is famous for cutting off

heads.

They take the photos up to the others but no-one remembers

taking the photo.

"I guess we believe what the photo says," suggests Carla.

"Believe the unbelievable".

"What if we took the orb?" says Holly half to herself.

The others look at her in astonishment. Nanna is doubtful. "It's an interesting idea…but…. Let's see what the orb thinks?"

They hurry down to the alcove. There's no sign of the orb.

"Not one of your better ideas, sis," declares Max.

Holly laughs. "You can say that again," she replies.

"Just the photos then," says Nanna. "Come on then or we'll be late and that would never do. We have our reputation to consider."

As usual they arrive right on time. Carla and Max leap out of the car eager to catch up with Louella and Ben. Before they can ring the bell, the door is flung open and not only Louella and Ben greet them but also their neighbours Simon and Curtis. Holly, bringing up the rear, gives a soft moan. The twins are a handful. Nanna flashes her a warning.

"Did you bring it? Did you bring it? demand the twins. They can hardly contain themselves.

"Bring what?" asks Max feigning ignorance. Louella gives him a sharp punch. He lightly punches her back

"Someone's been talking," laughs Carla. "Probably mum."

"Actually, it was your dad," replies Ben. "He was telling our parents."

Carla and Holly are astonished. "Dad? Really?"

"Well….. Is it true?" demands Louella.

Before they can answer, they are interrupted by John and Laura.

"Hi kids." Laura has barely time to greet Holly, Carla and Max before they are dragged away by her grandchildren.

"Hi Em and Henry." She gives them each a hug. John follows suite. "The kids are all abuzz. They've been waiting all morning for you to appear. Is it true? Did you bring it?"

John shakes his head in disbelief. "Don't be stupid Laura. It's just a story the kids have been fed by Matthew or…." he studies Nanna from under his eyebrows. "Emma?"

Laura looks disappointed. Nanna laughs. "Of course. Whatever you say John."

She links arms with Laura. "Are you going to invite us in or are we eating on the porch?"

Laura chuckles and ushers them in.

The children have disappeared into the family room. An excited murmur emanates from there.

John sorts out drinks for everyone and then takes Grandpa into the garden to light the barbecue. Nanna moves to follow Laura into the kitchen to help prepare the salads but her friend has half an ear on the conversation in the family room and when Holly dashes out and returns with the photos she can contain herself no longer. She moves close enough to the family room to be able to hear clearly. Nanna watches from the kitchen as Laura edges in closer and closer so that she can see the photos. She turns, realising she's being observed. She sheepishly rejoins her friend.

'What do you think? Nanna gives her friend an impish look. Laura eyes her suspiciously.

"How'd you do it?" she asks.

"That's my question," declares John, coming into the kitchen to collect the meat.

Nanna just raises her hands, shrugs and says, "You'll have to ask the children."

"A likely story," responds John. "How are those salads coming along? I'm putting the meat on now."

Nanna calls the children and they help the grandmothers carry the food into the garden. The table is set up under a large umbrella. They are all suddenly hungry. Grandpa rescues the meat before it's overcooked.

During lunch, the conversation keeps returning to the orb. The Parry children and the twins desperately want to see it. John tries to convince them it's a summer holiday entertainment prepared by Nanna. Carla and Max howl him down. They insist he looks at the photos. He suggests Nanna has created them in PhotoShop. Holly is affronted that he would think such a thing.

Louella hurries inside and fetches the photos from the family room. She checks them. They are bright and clear. She hands them to her grandfather.

As he takes them, he feels a strange vibration pass through his hands, down his legs and into his feet. The hairs on the back of his neck briefly stand on end as he looks at the photos. The paper is blank. He turns them over; nothing. He shows them and smirks. Louella snatches the photos from her grandfather. She turns them over. She turns them again. She can't believe it. They were there a moment ago. They're blank. She passes them around the table. The children are bewildered. Everyone starts talking at once. The twins jump up and down on their seats until John makes them stop. Laura stares at the blank pages. "I saw them before," she insists. "Someone must have switched them." She looks sternly at her husband.

"Not guilty, I assure you," is his answer. "Too busy cooking lunch. Perhaps they've **magically** faded," he suggests facetiously. "Or maybe the orb doesn't like me."

There is a sudden fierce gust of wind that erupts from nowhere. It shakes the umbrella and the plates on the table. There is a flash of light and the sun disappears, as if hidden by clouds.

The moment is frozen and then everything is back to normal. The children start talking, all at once. Grandpa laughs at the stunned expression on his friend's face. He claps him on the back and laughs. "Perhaps you're right, old boy." John grimaces at him ruefully.

"Oh my God!

Everyone turns to Laura as she drops the photos onto the table. She points frantically at one of the previously blank photos. In strong, bold, colourful text are the words;

'*Believe the unbelievable*'. She is speechless.

"Wow!" The children are ecstatic. Ben grabs the photo. He passes it around. "Gran's right," he declares.

John reaches forward to take it. He studies it suspiciously, looking from Nanna to Grandpa. He wags his finger at Nanna. "You've been up to something."

Nanna laughs. "Believe the unbelievable'," is all she says.

"Perhaps you'd like to ask it a question Pop," suggests Ben. His Grandfather waves him away with a laugh.

"I would Ben." says Laura, recovering from her fright. "How do you do it?"

"You ask," says Max. "Or sometimes you just think it."

"What would you like to ask Laura?" Nanna is curious.

Laura looks a bit sheepish. "Well," she counters. "If you think it really works, I'd like to know if I should retire."

"Good one, Gran," says Ben. "What about you, Pop?" When his grandfather doesn't respond, Ben calls out louder.

John looks up from the barbecue. He grins. "I'd like to know how Emma wangled all this nonsense." He is beset upon by all the children. They pin him down, tickling him and demanding he believe. He surrenders. "Okay. Okay. I believe."

Nanna laughs. "What do you believe, John?" They all wait.

"I believe the unbelievable," he gasps. "Now, let me up."

The children cheer and let him go.

When it's time to leave, Laura and John give them all a big farewell hug. John thanks them for a very entertaining afternoon. Laura and the children organise a time to visit and meet the orb. As they drive away, Laura calls out. "Let me know what it says." They wave in acknowledgement.

"That's presuming it's there when we get back," Carla reminds them.

Chapter 8

It is there, sitting comfortably in a soft green glow.
There's a new page and message.

"Listen to your heart and gut."

"I think that's for Laura," says Max. "It also answers some of the
other questions."

"I think so too," agrees Nanna, pleased by his perception. She
turns to Holly. "Have you remembered you promised to continue
the story, this evening?" Holly smiles and nods.

"Would you like us to come too?" asks Grandpa.

"If you like but I'll be okay. Perhaps Max and Carla might come.
We'll go after dinner".

Max and Carla eagerly agree to join her.

Nanna is happy with Holly's decision. It means she has come to
terms with the orb and her role in the story. The message is
spreading. She sends a text message to Laura with the orb's

response to her question. 'Listen to your heart and gut.' She wonders what Laura will make of it.

After dinner, the children and the dogs head down to the beach. It's another beautiful, still evening. Holly detects a faint green mist hanging in the bush. She points it out to the others. They decide it's a good omen.

A surprise awaits them at the beach. Several children are there to greet them. They were worried that Holly wasn't coming. They excitedly lead them along the beach to the caravan park.

A crowd, even bigger than the previous night, has gathered. The campers have set up a chair for Holly on the open lawn area and many people are already seated in a large semi circle. They wait patiently as she takes her place. Carla, Max and the dogs settle at the edge of the crowd.

Holly watches the soft green mist roll in from the beach and wrap itself through the crowd. She feels its energy all around her. There is absolute silence and a hushed expectancy as the crowd waits for her to continue the story. Even the sound of the sea seems to quieten. In her mind's eye she sees the story unravelling. The words just seem to form without effort. They flow from her mouth in beautiful prose. The crowd is mesmerised. The images seem to project into the evening sky. When Holly finishes, she studies the faces of the children and adults who've been hanging on to her every word. It's as if everyone is holding their breath.

She notices a small girl, of about six years, sitting close to the front. The girl is transfixed and very solemn. Holly leans forward, touches her fore finger to her mouth and whispers so that no-one else can hear. "Would you like to see it?"

The little girl's eyes open in awe. She nods and puts a finger to her lips. There is a tentative half smile.

Holly's voice is cocooned in a silent bubble that only the girl can hear. "Ask mummy or daddy to bring you tomorrow morning at seven o'clock,' she breathes. She points to the beach. "There's a track about two hundred meters along the beach; the house across the road at the top of the track. Wait at the gate." The little girl clasps her hands together and nods again. Holly blows her a kiss and stands up.

No-one moves as she, Max, Carla and the dogs leave the caravan park. They move in silence, even the dogs. There's only the sound of the sea, as they make their way along the beach and back up their track. The soft green mist keeps them company.

As they cross the road and open their gate, Carla finds her voice. "What did you say to that little girl, Holly?" Holly tells her. "What made you say that and why choose that girl?"

Holly shrugs. "I've no idea. In fact I don't have any idea what I said tonight. It just seemed to flow from me…. like someone else was speaking."

Carla and Max follow her through the front garden and in the side door.

"I wonder if she'll come." Max considers the idea out loud." I would "

"Come where? Who?" inquires Grandpa, coming downstairs to meet them at the alcove. The children pause for a moment, to check the orb, before responding.

The book is hidden in a soft blue mist that rises and falls like a gentle sea. It's the first time they have seen it like that.

"It's been like that for about twenty minutes." Grandpa ushers them upstairs. He and Nanna have been waiting, eager to hear how it all went.

They join Nanna in the lounge. Max gives a detailed account of everything that happened, including Holly's invitation to view the orb at seven, next morning. "It was awesome," he concludes. Carla agrees.

Nanna is intrigued by Holly's invitation. "What do you think, Holl? Will she come?"

Holly shrugs. "I guess we'll just have to wait and see."

Max is up first. He checks out the weather. The morning is overcast, windy and cool. "Typical," he mutters, "Good for the beach one day and then like winter the next."

He darts downstairs to check the orb. It still sleeps in its sea of tranquillity.

The dogs whine at the door. Max opens it but they want him to come into the garden. He follows them down to the front gate. The small girl is waiting there, tucked behind a man. Max frowns and checks his watch. It's only six thirty. Champ and Curly vigorously wag their tails.

"I know we're very early," apologises the man. "But Cindy insists the big girl said we had to come. She's been up since five...." His voice trails away. "My wife's looking after her brother and the baby. "You are expecting us, aren't you? We'll wait if...." The man is unsure.

Max recovers his manners. "Of course," he stammers. "Um, er, I'm Max." He opens the gate. "The dogs seem to like you, so come in."

The man gratefully guides his daughter into the garden. She clings to his leg. "James, Cindy's dad," He extends his hand. Max shakes it. He ushers the duo towards the house, not sure what to do. Fortunately Grandpa appears and suggests he go and get

Holly and Nanna.

Holly, sleepy eyed, is just emerging from the bathroom.

"They're here," hisses Max, grabbing her arm.

She shakes him off.

"Who? What?" Her mind clears. "You mean…. but it's only….."

"Yes! Grandpa is with them in the garden." Holly darts off to put

on some clothes while Max alerts Nanna and Carla. They quickly

make themselves presentable and follow Max back into the

garden where Grandpa and the two dogs are trying to make the

visitors welcome.

Cindy suddenly spots Holly. She rushes from her father's side

towards her. Holly kneels and gives her a hug. "Sorry I'm late.

I'm not known for being an early riser." She smiles at Cindy's

father and takes his daughter's hand. "Shall we go and look?" she

asks. Cindy hops up and down on the spot. "Yes, please," she

breathes.

Holly leads them into the house. They gather around the orb. It

sits in a mist of gold, green light. Cindy lets out a long sigh. Her face lights up and her eyes are filled with tears. "It is real," she whispers. "I knew it!" Her father kneels and wraps his arms around her. "Nick," said it wasn't real. He said I was making it up, as usual." She stands bewitched by the magic of it.

"Nick is her older brother," explains James. Like his daughter he is unable to take his eyes off the orb. The mist around it suddenly moves and a multitude of tiny stars swirl inside before clearing to reveal the small book. They watch in awed silence as it opens to a blank page.

"Would you like to ask a question?" asks Nanna gently. Cindy nods and takes a deep breath. Her soft voice trembles.

"Is Father Christmas real?" Her question takes them all by surprise. They wonder how the orb will respond. Carla, Max and Holly exchange doubtful looks.

Chapter 9

All eyes are on the orb as they wait expectantly for it to respond. At first there is nothing.

"Please," pleads Holly, under her breath. She glances at Cindy. The little girl's eyes are fixed on the orb and her hands are held up to her mouth. Cindy's eyes widen as a series of tiny stars flow from the orb towards her. She reaches out to touch them. They swirl all around her, enveloping her.

Later no-one can really explain what they saw. They only know something happened; something that left Cindy absolutely entranced and satisfied.

As the stars fade and the book closes, she reaches for Holly. "Thank you," she whispers. She places her pointer finger against her lips. Holly returns the gesture.

Cindy takes her father's hand and pulls it. "Come on daddy. Mummy's waiting for breakfast." Her father hastily offers his appreciation and thanks while his daughter drags him out. As they disappear through the front gate, Nanna, Grandpa and the three children burst into laughter.

Over breakfast they share their thoughts about what happened. Max and Carla think Cindy must have been drawn into the orb like they were but with a far more pleasurable outcome. Holly and Nanna think it was more a feeling experience. Grandpa has no idea at all. The time lapse was so short, how could anything take place? They all agree that whatever occurred, Cindy was very happy about it.

In the alcove a page turns.

The rest of the day is dull by comparison. The weather is not suitable for beaching so the children help their grandparents weed, trim and water the garden. Grandpa has a large vegetable patch and there are many vegetables to be picked. By late afternoon, they are all tired.

The weather is still overcast and threatening rain so while Grandpa walks the dogs, the children lounge about, checking their phone messages. They are completely taken by surprise by the number of text messages with requests to ask the orb a question; questions from the family, neighbours, friends and friends of friends. They ask Nanna what they should do. She suggests they discuss it with Grandpa when he returns. Meanwhile they could make a list of the questions.

She checks her landline phone. There's a voice message from Laura thanking her for the orb's lovely reply; she really understands it and the kids love it too and that John keeps finding a message, every hour, on his phone and computers. It says, 'believe the unbelievable'. Laura laughs on the phone and adds that "John says the joke's over and to ask Emma to stop please.' Nanna shakes her head in amusement. She wonders what it will take to make John believe. She shares the news with the children.

Nanna is cooking dinner when she hears Grandpa return. It sounds like he's talking to someone.

The children jump up, eager to get his opinion. He calls up the stairs. "Has anyone seen this last message? I think it's being funny." There's a mad rush downstairs to look. Holly is there first.

"My time not yours."

"How droll," giggles Holly. "It's got you pegged Grandpa."

He gives her a gentle wag of his finger. "It just explains the timing of what happened this morning," he replies, pretending to be stern.

"But you found the message," Nanna counters with a grin. The children clap in support. Grandpa laughs.

"Talking about time...... dinner's ready and waiting. We can ask Grandpa's opinion about what to do with all those questions you've received." Nanna leads the way back up stairs to the dining room.

After Nanna has replayed Laura's phone message for Grandpa and made him laugh, the children explain about all the text messages they've been receiving. They present the list of the requests. It's quite long. Grandpa listens carefully and considers the matter whilst he eats. He suggests perhaps they don't need to do anything more than write the questions down. However, as Carla points out, although they know the orb responds to thoughts and spoken words, they haven't tried it with written questions. Grandpa nods. "I don't think it matters. I'm sure the orb will work it out. It already decides what it will and won't answer. Let's leave the list pinned up somewhere and see what happens. Of course, even if it answers we may not know which question it's responding to."

"That's easy peasey," declares Max. We'll send everyone the same reply and they can interpret it any way they like….. or don't like" . He punches the air. "Easy peasey!"

It's quite late by the time they've resolved the issue. Before they go to bed, Carla uses a magnet to hang the list on the fridge. They check the orb one last time but nothing has changed. They say goodnight and head for bed certain that all is in hand.

107

None of them hears the dogs whine as the orb emits a deep hum into the night. The soft mist surrounding it turns deep blue and leaves the house, winding its way through the bush to the beach.

Chapter 10

Grandpa stirs in his sleep. Half awake, his conscious mind registers the sound of an extra large wave washing on to the beach, a signal that the tide is turning. He vaguely recalls that last night's tide was particularly high. He has a fleeting memory of a dream in which he was swimming with the whales. He has swum with the dolphins, whale sharks and manta rays but never with a whale. He'd love to swim with a whale.

In his dream he hears the whales calling. Suddenly he is wide awake. He hears the sound of a whale calling. He listens intently. There it is again. And then there is a softer reply. Careful not to disturb Nanna, he climbs out of bed and goes out on to the deck. It's still dark. The sky is clear and a full moon lights up the calm sea. He hears the whales call again. They sound distressed. He strains to see. Beyond the reef is a large swell in the calm of the surface of the sea. As he watches, the swell breaks and a dark shape arches out and back into the water.

Grandpa slips quickly inside to grab his binoculars. Even with the moon's light, it's hard to see clearly but he's convinced it's a whale. The shape breaks again and the moon catches the sheen of the water on its back. It is definitely a whale. It calls again and is echoed by a call closer to the beach and out of his view, which means it's in the inner channel. If the tide's out it may be beached.

He quickly wakes Nanna and explains to her what he thinks is happening. She suggests he goes to the beach, check it out and to ring her if help is required. He hurriedly dresses, grabs his mobile phone and finds his head light, so he can see in the bush. Then he collects a couple of buckets and a beach bag before heading down the track.

At the beach an upsetting sight greets him. In the moonlight he can see that a small whale has beached itself. Its mother is swimming offshore calling to it. Even though the inner channel is reasonably deep, the calf urgently needs help as it's wedged close to the beach.

Grandpa immediately phones Nanna. He asks her to rally the neighbours and friends and to bring as many buckets as possible. If they can keep the young whale calm and wet and the tide is as high as the previous evening they should be able to refloat it and then it could swim over the reef.

Leaving his phone and headlight in the beach bag and one bucket on the beach, he takes the other bucket and wades into the sea towards the whale. It struggles as he approaches and he murmurs soothing words to help calm it. Using the bucket, he starts sluicing it with water.

Nanna urgently wakes the children. Without hesitation they are up and dressed, eager to help. Carla and Max offer to go to the caravan park, while Holly volunteers to ring the 'Save the Whale Foundation'. Nanna will contact her local friends and neighbours. She reminds them to take their phones and torches. They can leave them in grandpa's beach bag if they go in the water. She makes a mental note to herself to keep the dogs in the house.

On his way out, Max catches sight of the orb. He briefly notices a new message.

"Hands of the universe".

But it doesn't make sense.

Halfway down the track it registers. Telling Carla to go ahead, he stops running and phones Nanna. She answers immediately.

"Nanna…. The orb… I noticed as I ran out… It says, 'Hands of the Universe'…." He pauses to catch his breath. Nanna admits she hasn't seen it as she's been busy contacting the neighbours, so he continues in a rush. "I think it means you've got to do Reiki …." His voice tapers off.

"Max, clever boy! Thanks. I'll be down soon."

Max breathes a sigh of relief and pleasure and races down the track to join Carla. Nanna hangs up and starts phoning her friends. They promise to meet her on the beach as soon as possible.

Meanwhile Holly has had no success with 'Save the Whale Foundation'. After being switched from one automatic message to another she decides to just leave a message. She and Nanna secure the dogs.

Several neighbours, armed with buckets, are waiting at their gate. They join Nanna and Holly and head down the track.

By they time they reach the beach, a small crowd has gathered. Carla, Max and several other people are helping Grandpa to douse the young whale. It is unresponsive, stuck on the sand. However the tide is on the way in and the water is already up to Grandpa's armpits.

Some spectators are getting in the way, edging closer all the time. Nanna quietly and firmly asks them to move back from the water and give the whale space. A couple from the caravan park offer to manage the crowd. She thanks them and hurries to join Holly and the neighbours.

"Emma! Emma!" Three of Nanna's friends have arrived. She indicates to Holly and the neighbours to go ahead and help with the watering while she brings her friends up to date and explains what she'd like to try. They wade into the water close to the head of the small whale. Nanna and her friends lay their hands on its side.

From the sea the mother whale calls to her calf.

The friends focus their thoughts. Nanna remembers the orb's words. 'I am the light of the universe. I am love'. She asks the universe to send its healing light of love to the whale.

She feels a tingle in her hands and a warm energy flow into the small whale. The vibrations and heat increase in strength. The others feel it too.

Grandpa and his band of helpers frantically pour buckets of seawater over the calf. For more than an hour they work. The sun rises at the far end of the beach. The water slowly gets deeper. The crowd grows but maintains its distance. The press arrive and then the police.

Suddenly the whale starts to tremble. Holly notices that the tide has crept in far enough to lap across the top of the beached whale. They continue with the hands on and the watering.

The reporters and the police are continually on their mobile phones calling for assistance. A helicopter swoops low over the scene; a television network team has arrived.

The tide rises up the beach, much higher than usual. The channel between the sand bank and the shore is now quite deep. The mother whale calls again. Grandpa feels the whale lift in the water. It gives an almighty heave. He shouts a warning as it humps. Push, he urges as the water rushes over it and under it. Everyone pushes harder. The whale trembles and humps again, moving further into the water.

Push! Push!

The whale gives a third huge tremor and slips further into the deepening channel. Grandpa directs the pushers to turn it to the right. Suddenly the whale is seaborne and on its way. Beyond the reef, the mother whale sounds over and over as her calf successfully crosses into the outer channel and joins her. It sounds like "Thank you."

The crowd on the beach is jubilant. They clap and cheer. TV cameras roll and reporters interview the spectators, keen to be on the news.

The children, Grandpa, Nanna and her friends gather their belongings and quietly slip away, up the track and back home. They are exuberant, so grateful and happy that they have been able to rescue the whale calf and reunite it with its mother. Breakfast sounds like a good idea.

As they pass the orb they stop. A new page is open with two words.

"Thank you."

"Thank you," they reply.

As the family and Nanna's friends sit on the deck and eat their breakfast, they contentedly watch the two whales head further out to sea and they discuss the series of events that culminated in the successful rescue.

After breakfast, Grandpa slips down to the beach to see what's happening. He hangs back at the edge of the track to avoid being noticed.

A large crowd still buzzes with excitement. People from 'Save the Whale Foundation', who have finally arrived, are stunned by the speed of the rescue. A television crew interviews many spectators. There's mention of a family and a girl who tells stories about an orb but no one is really sure what actually happened or who co-ordinated the rescue. The neighbours are also being asked questions.

Grandpa hastily returns to the house and reports back. He and Nanna decide it may be wise to take the children and the dogs out for the day to avoid any palaver or questions.

They thank and farewell Nanna's friends, pack a picnic and head for the hills. The children ring their mother on Nanna's car phone to share the excitement. They take turns to fill in the details. She is astonished and promises to let their father know. Grandpa cautions her about letting out too much information in case they are inundated with reporters. She laughs. "I thought you were meant to be the voice!"

"Not that much of a voice," replies her father. "I hope," he adds as an after thought.

The whale rescue makes headlines. It features on the TV midday news and the front page of the evening paper.

At first none of the family, nor their other friends, make the connection, although Grandpa and the children are quite prominent in the television footage and photographs. Apart from a couple of calls and texts from friends, asking for an eyewitness account, the evening is quiet.

The orb sits peacefully in a soft purple haze, on the leadlight cabinet, in the alcove. The book is closed.

Chapter 11

Early the following morning, when the children join their grandparents to say good morning to the orb, they are surprised to see a familiar page open. They re-read the words that had puzzled them previously.

"I am the words of the universe. You are the voice."

It makes even less sense and they ponder on it as they walk, with the two dogs, through the bush to the beach. Holly is a little concerned when she thinks about her mother's words from yesterday. She senses the green mist hovering in the trees. At least the beach is empty. The week-end holiday makers have all left and they are too early for the locals. The morning is fresh and it promises to be a beautiful, warm, sunny day.

Long rollers break on the reef. There is no sign of the whales but in the distance she sights a pod of dolphins and masses of diving birds. They are obviously following a school of fish.

119

Everything seems normal. She relaxes and joins her siblings in a run with the dogs. Nanna and Grandpa stroll, arm in arm behind them.

A surprise awaits them when they return home. A young newspaper reporter is waiting on the doorstep, anxious to interview them. The two dogs greet her with much wagging of tails. She kneels down and pats them. Grandpa asks what she wants. She explains she's been told they might be able to provide more information about the whale rescue.

"She's a bit early," grumbles Carla. "We haven't even had breakfast!"

The reporter gives her a regretful smile and apologises for being so early. Embarrassed, Carla mumbles and looks at the ground. Max punches her on the arm. She jabs him back. Holly recalls the words of the orb. She turns to her grandparents.

"Perhaps we could answer some questions, while we're having breakfast?" she asks. Nanna checks with Grandpa who nods in agreement.

They invite the reporter in and guide her upstairs to the deck, moving quickly past the orb.

The reporter waits patiently while they prepare the breakfast things, before she starts asking questions. Grandpa starts at the beginning. The children and Nanna fill in the missing pieces. The reporter makes notes on her phone. When they've finished, she sits still and studies them for a moment. Then she turns to face Holly.

"Are you the orb girl?" Holly blinks in surprise. She swallows and looks at Nanna for guidance. Nanna shrugs.

Holly is a little wary. She recalls the words of the orb; 'You are the voice.' "What do you mean?" she eventually asks.

The reporter explains that while they were interviewing people about the whale rescue there were reports of a girl telling wonderful stories about an orb being found on their beach and the magic it can do. She pauses for a moment before continuing to add that there's even a rumour that one of the children, staying at the caravan park, and her father actually saw the orb and had an experience. Holly waits in the silence that follows.

Grandpa cuts in. "Have you interviewed them?"

The reporter shakes her head. "They'd already left the caravan park."

Everyone looks at Holly. The words of the orb run around her head. She makes a decision. She likes the reporter. She sits up straight.

"Yes," she says. "I'm the orb girl." She pauses for effect. "Would you like to see it now or after we tell you the story?"

Nanna smiles.

The reporter is taken by surprise. She almost drops her phone. She decides to hear the story first.

They start from the beginning. The reporter sits and listens.

"Don't you think you'd better write this down? asks Max a little caustically.

"I'm er…. recording it," she awkwardly admits. "If that's okay…"

"It's probably a good idea," suggests Nanna. "At least it'll be accurate." Grandpa agrees.

They continue telling the story. When they finish, the reporter is totally mystified. She doesn't know whether to believe it or not. Nanna shows her the photos printed from the computer.

It's very compelling. The family watches as she sits in silence for a while, struggling to take it in. Finally she asks them if she can see the orb. They exchange quick smiles and take her downstairs to where the orb sits in its peaceful green glow; its pages closed. The reporter studies it carefully. Apart from the glow and the way the book hangs suspended, there appears to be nothing special about it.

It is a very strange story and she doesn't want to make a fool of herself but if it's real it's the story of a lifetime. She wonders to herself how she could test the truth. She senses a movement and blinks. The family holds its breath as they recognise the signs. The mist around the orb swirls to reveal a pink ribbon of light. There on an open page of the small, encased book are the words.

"The truth is in your heart."

The reporter's heart races and her eyes widen. Holly smiles.

"What were you thinking?" The reporter looks at her and then

123

quickly back to the orb as another page turns revealing another message.

"Always listen to your heart."

The story features in the evening paper.

More reporters arrive. A television crew and cameras roll in to film the orb. The family watches in fascination as the book remains closed. Disappointed the team leaves and interest wanes until a few days later another television unit arrives with a disgruntled Current Affairs anchorman from a popular evening show, who thinks he's wasting his time.

For the first time, Champ and Curly growl their disapproval. The children hide their amusement as he warily skirts around the dogs. He is surly. He spends most of the first hour scowling and grumbling as he asks questions, cynically views the photos and directs his film crew to film the orb from every angle.

The orb glows very faintly, a pale grey, but the book remains closed. Muttering about a waste of time and phoney claims, completely convinced they are on a wild goose chase, the presenter orders the crew to pack up. As they are leaving he glances back at the orb. It suddenly seems to glow brighter. Nanna observing with Holly, from the family room, notices too. She taps Holly on the arm. The presenter pauses.

Small red sparks fly from the orb towards him. He instinctively steps back. The orb glows brighter, red. Nanna and Holly are surprised. They've never seen the orb red. They watch as the presenter steps closer.

In a swirl of red mist a dark ribbon of light leads into the book. It opens to reveal one word.

"Smile."

Absolutely stunned the TV presenter turns to Nanna and Holly. They raise their eyebrows, give a gentle shrug and smile. He turns back to the orb. The word is clear.

"Smile."

Is it a trick? Neither the grandmother nor her grand-daughter was close enough to effect the change. It has to be for real. He gives a huge smile and a fist of joy. Hastily the film crew reassemble and start re-filming as the excited presenter explains to the camera what has just taken place. They film the orb again. Holly wonders if the film will actually be there when they want it.

The Current Affairs Programme puts the orb back in the headlines. Conjecture runs riot. Is it a hoax? Is it a magician's trick? Were they hypnotized? Is it a miracle?

Next day they are all invited to appear on a radio talkback show. Grandpa thinks only Holly and Nanna should go. He will stay at home with Carla, Max and the dogs. They promise to listen in. Before they go, Holly is very nervous. She talks with Nanna. Should they take the orb? What if they can't answer the listeners' questions? Nanna suggests she asks the orb for its advice. Its response is, as usual, fairly general. The pages turn rapidly.

"Look within for all answers.

Be yourself.

Keep it simple.

Go with the flow."

Holly makes a face at the orb. "Thanks for your help." The orb

seems to oscillate, its colours changing from red to green to blue.

Nanna laughs.

"You'll be right," she reassures her.

Holly feels a slight panic. She gives Nanna a strange look.

"What do you mean I'll be right?"

"You're the messenger, remember." Holly turns pale. "But I'll be

here with you all the way." She gives Holly a huge hug. "Let's

go; just you and me. I'm sure the orb will be with you some

how."

There is a warm welcome at the radio station. The radio presenter

is really enthusiastic and supportive. He settles them into their

headphones and invites them to tell their story.

Nanna leaves it all to Holly. She goes 'with the flow' and narrates

their story. She feels completely at ease, like she did in the

caravan park. The presenter interrupts every now and then with a

question. At one point, Nanna explains how the responses from

the orb often appear to be directed to the unconscious mind rather than the conscious one. Therefore it's better not to try to analyse too much. When Holly is finished, the presenter invites his listeners to phone in.

Immediately the radio station's switchboard is jammed with callers. Holly feels totally relaxed and confident. Answers just flow from her. Nanna lets her do all the talking. Not even the antagonists and sceptics disturb her calm. She lets her unconscious mind flow, feeling what the orb would say.

Time flies.

Holly is amazed to discover they've been on air for over an hour. The programme presenter is overjoyed with the results. He asks one last question.

"What is your best advice?'

Holly doesn't hesitate. The song plays in her head. "Imagine", she replies. The presenter nearly falls off his chair. He looks at her in amazement and then speaks into his microphone.

"We'll take a short break." He switches on the music and removes his headphones. The familiar music and lyrics of John Lennon's 'Imagine' fill the studio. Nanna and Holly exchange smiles.

So great is listener response that Holly agrees to take on a regular weekly session for the rest of the holidays.

Further invitations to appear on radio and television roll in. She agrees to as many as possible, as long as Nanna can come too.

Chapter 12

A few days later, on a dull, cloudy morning, Grandpa awakes to the sounds of the dogs barking. It's barely daylight. He walks out on to the upstairs deck. A crowd is gathered outside the front gate, deterred from entering by Champ and Curly. Someone calls to him to show them the orb. He isn't sure what to do. He wakes Nanna.

"Em, they're demanding to see the orb," he whispers.

Half asleep, Nanna peers out through the window.

She is staggered. "Oh my goodness!" She jumps up, suddenly wide awake. "We'd better wake Holly."

After they slip into their tracksuits, Nanna wakes Holly while Grandpa checks the orb. The book is closed.

The men, women and children in the crowd start to chant. They want Holly and the orb. Grandpa hesitates and then picks it up and carries it upstairs to where Holly and Nanna are waiting.

Max and Carla sleepily struggle from their bedroom. Grandpa explains what is happening, while Holly with Nanna takes the orb out on to the deck. Holly places the orb on the hand rail.

The crowd grows silent in anticipation, straining at the gate, wanting to enter but held back by the dogs. From the bush behind rises the soft green mist. It crosses the road and the dogs withdraw. The mist weaves its way around the crowd, gathers them together and gently herds them through the gate to stand directly beneath the deck. To the east a heavy bank of clouds suddenly parts and a brilliant shaft of sunlight pierces the eucalyptus trees in the bush to illuminate Holly, Nanna and the orb. The mist settles lightly on the crowd. The garden appears to brighten and burst into bloom. You can hear a pin drop.

Grandpa, Carla and Max watch from inside.

Holly feels nervous. She wonders how to handle this.

A page of the book turns. Holly hesitates and then reads its message out loud.

"Accept responsibility for your actions."

The words echo through the mist.

For a few moments the crowd is silent. Then it erupts in a chorus of questions. Holly draws back, unsure what to do next. Nanna feels the energy and words of the orb flow through her, guiding her.

"Meditation is the key."

Nanna takes control. Her voice is soft and gentle yet it reaches everyone as she leads the men, women and children standing below her in a meditation. Trance like, they follow her imagery into a place of silence and clarity. The mist wraps them in a cloak of peace. Within the orb the mist turns to pink and the pages of the book turn. Nanna nods to Holly and Holly reads each message out aloud as it appears.

"Tune into your thoughts.

What do you think about?

Your thoughts shape you.

Thoughts are powerful.

You become your thoughts."

Throughout the reading, the soft green mist softly caresses the crowd. Gradually it starts to lift and drift back to the bush. The clouds close over and the shaft of light almost disappears. Finally the pages of the book close. The people in the crowd stand motionless, waiting. At last they recognize that the audience is over. They start to move off but stop as the orb unexpectedly turns one last page. Holly reads the words.

"Believe in miracles."

The crowd releases one large collective sigh, then quietly disperses.

Holly returns the orb to its sanctuary and the family go about their day wondering what further amazing things are in store for them.

They don't have to wonder for long. The next morning there is an even larger crowd waiting for them. Fortunately they are awake and dressed early. The crowd fills the garden and overflows into the street. Traffic in the nearby streets is brought to a standstill. There is neither mist, nor shaft of sunlight but the crowd is still eager to see the orb and ask it questions.

Again Holly brings the orb to the deck. Again Nanna prepares to lead the meditation. She hesitates. How will they hear her? She gestures to Max who immediately grasps the situation. He darts back to the family room and finds the karaoke microphone. Armed with the microphone, Nanna easily guides the crowd through a meditation. This time she asks them to each think of a question.

For an hour Holly and the orb respond. Holly has no idea what questions are asked but the members of the crowd appear satisfied. At the end of the hour she closes the session and just like the day before the crowd quietly disperses.

For the next three mornings the crowd numbers continue to grow. They meditate; ask questions in their heads, listen and leave. Each day the orb's last words are always the same.

"Believe in Miracles."

Once more the orb makes headline news. At the shops, Holly and Nanna are besieged by friends and strangers, wanting to ask questions. The phone runs hot until Grandpa decides to unplug it.

Holly, Carla and Max are inundated with text messages.

FaceBook is rampant with accounts of first hand experiences, speculation and fabrication.

The children change their mind about wanting to be famous.

People are hanging around the front gate all day. Fortunately Champ and Curly deter them from actually coming in. The family feels trapped inside.

Just before dinner, when the crowd has dispersed, they sneak out through the neighbour's garden to go for a walk. Luckily, the neighbour is away. They deliberately avoid the beach. During their walk Grandpa discusses his concerns about the next morning. So far the crowd has been respectful of their property but with the increasing numbers, it could get out of hand.

They decide to contact the police. This is a fortunate decision.

A car and two police officers arrive at dawn the following morning. The crowd is already twice as big as the previous day and a little restless as many people are a long way from the action. They push and jostle in an endeavour to get closer. The police have difficulty controlling them. They call for reinforcements.

Holly waits nervously at the side of the deck, out of view.

The orb is already on the rail. She wishes that the mist would rise from the bush and weave its magic calm over the crowd.

She is so focussed on the crowd that when she feels a hand on her shoulder she jumps. Max has crept up beside her.

"Look!" he whispers excitedly pointing at the orb. "The mist...."

Holly follows his direction. The mist, a deep mauve, is winding its way from the orb out on to the deck. She feels a strong sense of relief as it moves towards them and wraps itself around her. She squeezes Max's arm in thanks and, as Nanna joins her, moves to the rail and faces the crowd. The mist moves with her. The appearance of the mist stuns the crowd into silence.

The police officers survey the scene in astonishment, amazed at the sudden change. The crowd now waits expectantly, eager to be led into the magic. Nanna begins, as usual, with a meditation and an invitation to think of a question. Holly waits for the pages to turn. Nothing happens. She taps the orb. It flares momentarily but offers no advice. Nanna sees the panic flare in her eyes.

She points at Holly and whispers. "You.... you know what to say." As Nanna holds the crowd in a trance, Holly swallows and takes a deep breath. She allows herself to relax into the mist. Only one thought comes to her. She relays it to the crowd.

"Act for the highest good."

She waits for more but there's only the usual final message.

"Believe in miracles."

The session is over and everyone quietly leaves.

Grandpa thanks the police officers for their assistance. They express their appreciation for being able to witness the whole amazing scene.

Later in the morning Holly is due to make her next radio appearance. What if there's a crowd waiting for them there? Grandpa phones the producer of the show to discuss the situation. She suggests he drop Holly and Nanna off at the rear entrance and she gives him the directions.

Holly's heart is in her mouth as they approach the radio station building. They check the front entrance first. A huge crowd has gathered at the front entrance. Holly and Nanna duck their heads as Grandpa makes a quick detour. The producer greets them at the back door and leads them through a series of corridors to a rear studio.

"We thought it would be wiser to run it here today," she explains. The presenter is already in the booth. He gives them the thumbs up while he plays some introductory music.

Even before he introduces Holly, the switchboard is jammed. He suggests they start the session like they have been doing each morning, with a meditation and then Holly can answer some questions. After an hour Holly is exhausted. Even though the questions are completely different her answers are always the same.

"Accept responsibility for your actions.

Act for the highest good."

Despite this, the listeners are happy and just want more.

The presenter and producer are delighted with the session and beg Holly and Nanna to continue next week.

Grandpa is waiting in the car, with Carla and Max, in the street at the back door, to take them home. Because of the crowd waiting outside their front gate, they park in the next street and sneak in through the neighbour's garden.

People begin to talk about the orb and miracles in the same breath.

Chapter 13

Suddenly people in higher places start to take an interest in Holly and her orb.

Later that evening, when they are relaxing, watching television, the front door bell rings. Champ and Curly immediately jump up and race downstairs, barking furiously. Grandpa asks if anyone is expecting visitors but no-one is.

Followed by Max, he quietly follows the dogs. The bell rings again causing the dogs to bark even louder. Grandpa switches on the outside light and making sure the safety chain is on, he cautiously half opens the door. Three men are waiting, caught like startled rabbits in the sudden light.

The front man is large and showy. Grandpa recognises him as the local Member of Parliament. Reassured, he opens the door further. Behind the MP is a priest and bringing up the rear is a slim man, in a grey suit. The three men take a nervous step back as the dogs start to growl threateningly. Max takes hold of their collars and restrains them.

The local Member of Parliament steps forward, offers his hand to Grandpa and with assurance introduces himself.

"Damian Carver, local MP…" He points to the priest. "Father Diavola and …. Er …. Mister…… er…." He hesitates, momentarily at a loss. "Ah yes…. Reeman." He gives him a strange look.

"With a y" adds the third man with a quiet smile. The priest says nothing.

There's an uncomfortable silence. Champ and Curly continue to growl.

Grandpa breaks the silence. "And how can we help you? It **is** rather late."

The MP apologises profusely for the lateness of their visit. He explains that they've been asked to urgently check out the orb, as some people are worried about its growing influence.

"Really?" Grandpa wonders to himself who 'some people' are but he smiles politely. "And what would you like to check out?"

"Well…. Perhaps we could see it…." the politician's voice trails off. "… you know… to see if it's real…."

"Of course it's real." Max is indignant. "Do you think we're scammers?" He moves as if to free the dogs.

The MP hastily reassures him that that's not what they think. Neither of the other men says a word.

Grandpa decides to check with Nanna and Holly. He suggests the men wait outside while he consults with his wife and granddaughter. He closes the door firmly and he and Max take the dogs back up to the lounge where Nanna, Holly and Carla are waiting, curious.

"Who is it? asks Holly. Grandpa describes the men and their mission.

"How do we know they're for real?" Holly is suspicious

"Curly and Champ aren't too keen on them." adds Carla. Max agrees.

Grandpa explains that he recognised the MP. "What do you think Holl? Should we let them in?"

Holly looks around the group, unsure. Nanna laughs.

"They'll just be back tomorrow if we don't let them in now so we might as well. Let's all go and see what the orb has to offer. Perhaps it can help."

They leave the dogs in the lounge and troop downstairs. Grandpa invites the men in and introduces them to the rest of the family. Nanna notices that when Grandpa introduces Holly, the priest stares at her, dark eyes cold, under hooded lids. She has a fleeting image of a vulture. The third man only nods.

"Well! Where is it then?" demands Damian Carver, keen to take back the initiative. "We don't want to keep you folk up all night" The three children look at him in disbelief. The orb's not going to like him. Nanna gives them a knowing grin and leads the way. The orb is sitting very quietly at rest. There is just a faint suggestion of mist within the orb but the book isn't visible. It really just looks like a glass ball. The MP presses closer, unimpressed. It's obviously not what he expected.

"Is it always like this?" he enquires. "I thought it had a book in it and coloured mist swirling in and out and bright lights....and ..."

The orb remains still. Holly thinks it's shining less brightly than usual. The priest and the man in grey, watching from a distance, say nothing.

"It has," affirms Max, "but sometimes it doesn't like people." He stares pointedly at the men.

The MP gives his politician laugh and assumes a sweet avuncular air. "Tell us all about it then. And what about the miracles?"

The priest groans but says nothing. Nanna suggests they move into her office so they can sit down.

Holly starts at the beginning, giving a brief outline and the others help fill in the spaces. They omit any mention of their own personal experiences. They have no confidence in the integrity of the men. The man in grey, whose rank they never catch, takes copious notes. They show the men their photos from that first day. None of them makes any comment. They simply stand up and return to the alcove where they study the orb carefully from all sides.

During their absence the book has become visible. Its appearance is so subtle that the men wonder if it was there all the time and they just didn't notice it.... or perhaps they've forgotten.

To the family the orb seems to have become even dimmer, a dull version of its usual self. The lights on the cover of the book are dull and flat.

"How does it work girlie?"

Holly jumps at the unexpected question fired at her by the priest. His eyes bore into her. She closes hers, takes a breath and then very slowly exhales. "We don't know. We just ask or think questions and if it chooses it replies with words on a page of its book. Sometimes I just hear the words in my head."

She pauses to see if there's any response from him. None. But when she relates its first answers to their questions about what it is, the priest looks disturbed. In sharp tones he questions her memory and accuracy.

At this, Nanna intervenes. She smiles gently and calmly produces a small book from the cabinet on which the orb sits. She explains that she keeps a record of the orb's words. She reads some of the words from her book, the orb's answers to some of their questions.

Is it theirs to keep? 'Yes.'

What are you? 'I am the light of the universe.'

What is the light of the universe? 'Love.'

Where does the love come from? 'The heart of the universe.'

What did it mean? Why had they found the orb or had it found them? 'I am the words of the universe. You are the voice.'

Carla adds one more, emphatically addressing her words to the MP. "There are no miracles, Mr Carver. The orb keeps saying 'Believe in miracles.' People are making the miracles bit up."

Grandpa gives her a thumbs up.

Nanna closes her book.

They all study the reaction of the three men. The politician is openly cynical, the priest on his guard and the third man suddenly alert.

"Perhaps you'd like to ask a question." Holly suggests.

The politician vigorously shakes his head. The grey man defers

to the priest who hesitates for a moment, gives a nervous cough

and then in a flat voice, totally devoid of any emotion asks the orb

where it came from. For a second the orb glows but then it fades.

The book remains firmly closed.

The priest repeats his question but there is still no response from

the orb. The politician gives a dismissive snort. He asks Holly

why there's no reply. She replies that she isn't sure. Perhaps the

question hasn't come from the heart or maybe the questioner

doesn't really want to know the answer.

She gives an apologetic smile to the priest. He gives her a strange

look and mutters something about witches.

"May I hold it, Holly?" The grey man has a soft musical voice.

His question diverts the attention away from the priest. For an

instant, the orb glows and Holly nods. The other two men watch

closely for they too had noted the strange halo of light that had

momentarily flared. He picks up the orb and turns it over and

around in his hands. He appears puzzled by its material and

structure and intrigued by the way the book is suspended in space in the centre of the orb and the manner in which the orb seems to flatten when placed on a surface. In his hands it is perfectly round and rigid and there appears to be no way of accessing the book. He finds it strangely exciting and thinks it warrants further examination. If only the book would open.

He holds it out to the MP and the priest but they both draw back from it. He comes to a decision. There's only one thing to do. They have to take the orb with them for further scientific examination!

He replaces the orb on the cabinet, pulls his cohorts to one side and hastily consults with them. They agree. They also want the photos and the diary.

When the MP relays this news to the family, they are speechless. How dare they! Holly's heart is in her mouth. She wonders if this is what the orb wants. She suddenly feels the men tense and quickly turns back to the orb. The pages of the book flicker.

Flecks of light sparkle on its cover. Then it is still. Holly knows in her heart what the orb wants.

She finds her voice. "It's okay." Her grandparents and siblings look doubtful. She re-assures them. "I'm sure."

Nanna finds a box and Holly carefully wraps the orb in wool. Then she releases the orb with love into the care of the grey man. He promises to look after it and to keep them informed. Nanna hands the MP a copy of their photos but she refuses to hand over her diary.

When the three men have gone, despite the late hour, they collect all their torches and walk down to the beach, taking in the beauty of the plants, the sand, the sea and the night sky and letting its peace envelop them. They stop for a moment, in silence, at the spot where they had found the orb. They delay returning home, not wanting to see the empty space where the orb has rested. They speculate on what might happen next. Will the orb be returned to them? They review some of the messages the orb had sent them;

to think positively, to expect the best and most of all to believe in miracles.

"What about tomorrow's crowd? There's no orb." Max brings them back to the practicalities of the present. They consider the situation but as Carla points out Holly usually knows what to say, even without the orb and that she doesn't even take it to the radio station so they decide to play it by ear.

They return home to a most wonderful sight. There in the space where the orb sat is a very faint, soft glow of golden light. The essence of the orb is still there. They feel their spirits lift.

Next morning an extra large crowd is waiting for them. Nanna explains that the orb had been taken away for scientific study. An angry murmur runs through the crowd but she calms them and reminds them of the orb's words; to believe in miracles. She tells them that she's sure that the orb wants them to continue asking questions, that the spirit of the orb is still here and will provide the answers. The crowd responds with an intensity that surprises her and they have a most incredible session. Even without the orb the answers flow from Holly.

Days go by with out any word. Grandpa rings Damian Carver but he has little news, only that 'specialists' are examining the orb. He won't or can't provide a telephone number for the grey man. They continue to conduct their morning sessions with ever increasing numbers and Holly continues with her regular radio segment. Callers become more and more incensed by the government's lack of response and its decision to take possession of the orb. Holly offers them words from the orb.

"Be tolerant, patient and understanding.

Expect the best."

"Believe in Miracles.

Current Affairs programs keep the orb in the spotlight by rerunning original footage of the orb story. Even their reporters are unable to access information on the progress or nature of the investigation. They demand action.

Two weeks after the men have taken the orb a spokesperson from the National television station rings Holly to advise her that the Minister of Science will make a statement to the press, live, that evening on the news. He asks if she'd be happy to have a news team present as they watch the report. She consults with Nanna and Grandpa. As they've heard nothing and have been unable to contact any of the three men, they agree and a television unit arrives shortly before the news commences. Ratings go off the board.

The family, including Matthew and Amanda who have come down to support them, hold their breath as the Minister for Science, facing a sea of reporters, nervously begins to speak. He apologizes for the delay but explains that despite all tests and experiments they are unable to shed any light on the source or authenticity of the orb. They are unable to open it and access the book. The book will not respond to any of their questions, which fails to give credence to the stories about its messages. However, there appears to be no way in which it could be externally manipulated and its ability to hang suspended within the orb is way beyond any known science. The material and construction of the orb are also technically beyond our current knowledge.

The minister concludes by announcing that further tests are to be undertaken as it is important to determine the true origins of the orb. In the meantime the orb will be kept under guard in the Natural Science Museum where it will be available for daily public viewing.

He folds his notes and prepares to leave but a barrage of questions and accusations from the reporters, about the legalities of the government's actions, lack of consultation and the rights of the orb's owners hurl him back into his seat. Does the government really believe there is something mystical about the orb or is it just taking advantage of its current popularity and newsworthiness?

The minister's colour rises as he assures the reporters and viewers that everything is under control and being properly handled, everything is going through the proper channels.

Then as the television cameras switch to their home, panning to the place where the orb has rested, the news anchorman asks whether or not the owners of the orb have been consulted or kept up to date. The cameras focus on Holly as the minister fumbles his reply in the affirmative.

The family sit in stunned disbelief? They have been unable to speak to anyone in authority about the fate of the orb and certainly haven't been consulted about its new role.

Holly listens to the minister again assuring the viewers that everything is being done correctly. She is puzzled by the orb's lack of response. Surely this is a most opportune time to spread its word. Had it no premonition that this would happen or is it all part of a larger plan? She realizes that the reporter is asking for her response to the minister's statements. For a moment she thinks to hotly refute his affirmations but then she sees the orb's words.

"Speak ill of no-one.

If you give criticism, you'll receive it in return."

Believe in miracles."

She realises that the minister is the messenger just as she is. She wonders what the orb would want her to say. She listens to her heart as the orb has taught her. Then she looks into the camera and smiles sincerely and quietly states that she is sure that the government has the highest good in mind and will accept responsibility for its actions. She accepts that whatever her role is to be she is willing to play it. She and her family are committed to the truth behind the words of the orb. She concludes with the words from the orb.

"Keep an open heart and mind.

Start each day with new hope.

Live one day at a time.

Trust in the flow."

Believe in miracles."

The camera swings back to the minister to gauge his reaction.

His look of relief makes Holly pleased that she has not discredited him.

Now the media really has something to get their teeth into. That night, the Current Affairs Shows have a field day. Debate rages as to the moral rights of the government to confiscate the orb. Nothing the family says will deter them. They have their controversy and will not let go.

The family is overwhelmed by the reaction. The phone rings ceaselessly until the answering machine is full. Again Grandpa unplugs it. No-one feels like answering. Close friends text to give support. Amanda and Matthew decide to stay the night. The children are delighted. They bring them up-to date with tales of the orb. Their parents advise them that the renovations are nearly finished and they'll be able to return home before the end of the holidays. The children aren't sure if this is good or bad news. The peace and quiet might be nice but….. They avoid watching the late news services and go to bed early.

The response is staggering. They can hardly believe it possible but the morning crowd, assembled outside the front gate, has doubled. The air is charged with electricity. Holly feels it vibrate through the deck rails. Her parents, as they watch from inside the

156

house, are flabbergasted by the size of the crowd and absolutely amazed by Holly's ability to cope with the whole situation. She appears so calm and relaxed, standing there next to Nanna.

Holly looks down at the crowd and wonders what to say. The crowd is so silent it's surreal. She feels their unspoken questions but no words came to her. Even Nanna is speechless.

Suddenly a small child pushes through the crowd and starts to open their gate. She stops uncertainly as the two dogs move towards her. Then she gives a huge smile and throws her arms into the air as she calls out, "We love you Holly!"

The crowd respond with spontaneous applause and echo the words, "We love you Holly!"

Holly is so choked with emotion she can't speak. Tears well in her eyes and roll down her cheeks. She turns towards Nanna to find that she too is emotionally overcome. Turning back to the crowd she gives a slight bow of acknowledgement and they go indoors.

The crowd seems to just melt away.

The children spend the rest of the day shopping with their parents while Nanna and Grandpa take the dogs and visit some friends. Matthew and the children are cooking a special dinner. Before dinner they all take the dogs for their usual evening walk.

It's one of those magical evenings when the sea is like glass, reflecting the delicate colours of the sky. The setting sun, a large brilliant ball of red, flicks light clouds with pastel fingers of gold, rose and peach as it dips into the sea. They watch the twilight deepen into mauve and violet before they climb the track home. Dinner is a sensation, eight courses, including crayfish. It's like something off a television show. Amanda, Nanna and Grandpa heap high praise on Matthew and the children. They tidy up while the children relax with their dad.

The wonders of the day however are not yet done. They watch with amazement as the evening television news shows a never ending queue of people waiting to view the orb which is now housed in an elevated glass case, behind a rope barrier.

When their house phone rings, Nanna answers it. She is staggered to hear her youngest daughter in England report that they've just featured on their morning news.

The orb has now gone international. Whatever next!

The number of people queuing to see the orb continues to grow. They come from all walks of life and all age groups. They all have questions to ask but the orb remains silent. The book is barely visible, dull and lifeless.

More and more powerful lobby groups, for and against the orb, spring into action. Supporters demand that the orb be returned to its rightful owner. Argument rages as to who is the rightful owner.

Nanna and Grandpa try to keep things as normal as possible but it is difficult. The morning crowds no longer come. Instead they are bombarded by representatives of the various action groups, demanding to speak to them and especially Holly. Some ask their opinion on the state of things, some accuse them of fraud and some urge them to demand the orb be returned.

Finally they decide it'll be best if the children return home, where hopefully, they'll have some privacy and peace. The children spend the day packing and tidying and then Nanna and Grandpa take them home.

They are delighted with the renovations and for a while forget about the dramas of the orb. They realise that there are only two weeks left before school resumes but it's a good idea not to dwell on that. Nanna and Grandpa stay for an early dinner and then return home to Curly and Champ. Before leaving, they promise to let them know if they hear anything.

For the next few days the children try to get back to normal. With their mother, they focus on preparing for the new school year. There are books to collect and uniforms that they've outgrown. They try to avoid places where they're known but it's not always possible. In the end, Holly finds it easier to stay at home, away from the inevitable questions and requests for help. Some people even want to touch her.

Each evening she talks to Nanna for any updates. Apart from the glow in the alcove occasionally brightening, Nanna has no news. The media maintains a regular surveillance of the orb and the endless procession of people.

Nanna and Grandpa also try to settle back into routine. The house is very quiet without the grandchildren. The glow of light in the alcove provides proof that the past few weeks were real. They walk the dogs and Grandpa works in their beautiful garden and helps a couple of friends in theirs, while Nanna paints or sees clients for reiki or hypnosis.

Each day she sits in the garden and meditates. Her clients are supportive and curious. They ask many questions about the fate of the orb. Nanna tells them that they probably know as much as she does. There is no word from the government. They can only wait and trust.

The orb has been on display for almost a week, when things take a dramatic turn. Despite the thousands of questions it has been asked there has been no response, not even a flicker of light. The book sits flat and lifeless within it. The media and the crowd are becoming frustrated and impatient. Those people interviewed by the press express their disappointment and many are starting to think it's a hoax.

On the morning of the seventh day, among the people queued up to see the orb is a young boy and his father. The boy clings anxiously to his father's leg as they are pulled and jostled by the mass of people. The queue moves slowly. When, at last, they stand before the orb the small boy suddenly lets go of his father and slips under the rope barrier. Before his father or the guards can react, he asks the orb a question. His question, barely more than a whisper, comes straight from his heart.

'Is mummy in heaven?'

The orb responds instantly. It glows brightly; the mist swirls and reveals a path in to the book. The book opens and a page turns to display a single word.

"Yes."

A brilliant smile lights the boy's face and brings tears to his

father's eyes. The guards, waiting to remove him, pause.

A murmur of excitement runs through the crowd. Here is the

moment they've been waiting for! They push forward as the boy

asks a second question. 'Where's heaven?' Again the orb

responds immediately.

"Heaven is in the heart of the universe, in your heart."

The boy whispers a quiet thank you and scurries back to his

father. As the crowd surges, the father gathers his son into his

arms and safely slips away. The guards strain to hold the people

back.

There is pandemonium. Museum security calls for

reinforcements. The word 'miracle' ripples through the crowd.

Everyone wants to be a part of the action. Reporters urgently

communicate with their editors. News flashes interrupt radio and

television programmes. Television crews and more reporters

converge on the museum. A host of eyewitnesses become instant

celebrities.

Grandpa catches the news flash as he is driving home from the shops. As soon as he reaches home he rushes inside and turns on the television. He calls for his wife but then remembers she is with Holly and Amanda who have driven up to the radio station.

Holly, in the middle of her weekly radio session, today with a live audience, suddenly stops talking, as a blaze of light flares before her eyes. An image of the incident flashes before her. She gives a gasp of wonder and turns with excitement to Nanna and the show's compere and blurts it out.

At that same instant the compere's monitor reveals the news that the orb has spoken. The compere is thunderstruck not sure of what he's hearing. The audience is stunned. Hands shoot up everywhere, demanding to ask a question. Seconds later a breathless reporter bursts into the studio and confirms the news. The studio is abuzz. Again the word 'miracle' hangs in the air. Amidst the chaos, Nanna and Holly make a hasty exit through the rear entrance and sprint to the car. Amanda, unable to escape through the ensuing confusion, texts Holly to say she'll meet them back at Nanna's house.

As the pandemonium subsides, Amanda, who has fortunately maintained a low profile, is able to push her way through the studio audience. She heads for her parents' house, collects them, Holly and the dogs and takes them home. The media hasn't sourced their address yet so they should be able to avoid the immediate drama.

The newspapers and television have a field day. Headlines run riot. 'ORB SPEAKS!' 'ORB MIRACLE!' 'ORB PROOF!' Major overseas networks take up the story. Even without the father and his son, who wisely remain anonymous, there are plenty of eyewitnesses, government and church leaders and paranormal 'experts' to interview. The debate intensifies.

As Holly can't be contacted, her on-air revelation is played over and over.

Nanna and Grandpa decide to stay a couple of days with their children and grandchildren and wait for things to quieten down.

They follow the events on television. Security at the museum is doubled. Crowd numbers viewing the orb continue to rise. The orb however is again dormant.

Two evenings later, they return home. They are relieved to find no reporters on the doorstep.

As they enter the house they notice that the usual very faint glow where the orb had sat is gone. Nanna is surprised but not worried. She says her usual goodnight to the orb before she goes to bed.

Chapter 14

Holly is dreaming about the orb, dreaming that it has returned. In her dream, she is at Nanna's and Grandpa's house. She can see a faint light under her bedroom door. She quietly walks around the bed and onto the landing. Sure enough the light is coming up the stairwell. She feels herself tingle all over. Is someone there? She carefully tiptoes downstairs. A magical sight greets her. The orb is in its special place in the hallway. Its glow is brighter than she can ever remember and the book cover vibrates in a kaleidoscope of colours. She feels her heart swell with love until she thinks it will burst. The dream disappears and she wakes suddenly, taking a moment or two to work out where she is. She leaps out of bed and rushes into her parents' bedroom. She urgently shakes her mother.

"Mum. Mum. Wake up." Her mother struggles to wake. She peers at the clock. It's only 5:30.

Holly shakes some more. "We've got to go to Nanna's. It's back."

Holly is very insistent.

Nanna wakes suddenly. She wonders what has disturbed her

sleep. The dogs bark and the doorbell rings. She checks the clock

and groans. It's only 5:30.

Grandpa wakes as the doorbell rings again. He slips on his

dressing gown and staggers downstairs, closely followed by his

wife. Keeping the security chain on, he opens the door. Nothing

could have prepared them for the shock of seeing two policemen

waiting outside, with Champ and Curly hovering close beside

them. Grandpa releases the chain and lets them in. The sergeant

introduces them both and apologises for the early intrusion.

"We've come to check on the orb," he explains.

"The last we heard, it's in the Science Museum." Nanna raises her

eyebrows at Grandpa and makes a small moue with her mouth.

"Not now..... er .... It's been stolen..... ".

Both policemen are discomfitted. "We thought it might be

here....." adds the constable.

Nanna and Grandpa are dumbfounded. They stare in disbelief.

"Stolen! Stolen?" Nanna finds her voice first.

"And you think we might have had something to do with that?" Grandpa emphasises the 'we'.

The policemen have the grace to look embarrassed.

"Sorry sir …. We have instructions to look". The sergeant lifts his hands and shrugs.

Grandpa smiles in sympathy. "In that case, you'd better have a look."

He leads them into the alcove. "It's usually here but as you can see there's just the cabinet….. and we've been here all night."

As the policemen stand awkwardly in the alcove, unsure what to do next, Nanna laughs and adds, "Perhaps you'd like to search the house…." They assure her that that won't be necessary, apologise profusely for the inconvenience and sheepishly leave.

"We'd better check the news Em." Grandpa lets Champ and Curly in and heads upstairs.

The television news is filled with the story. Apparently there are no signs of breaking and entering at the museum. After the recent revelation, security had been doubled. There are no clues as to how it was taken nor where it might be. The museum is highly embarrassed. The government is furious. Who could have stolen it and why?

Suddenly they hear the sound of a car door slamming. The dogs leap up, tails wagging and race down stairs. Nanna and Grandpa follow them. Holly rushes past them into the house.

"Is it here?" A bemused Amanda tags behind her. "We had to come. She was insistent." Her father laughs in disbelief.

"Don't tell me you think we stole it too." He teases her. His daughter looks surprised.

"Stolen? What do you mean?"

"Haven't you heard….?" Before they can continue the discussion there is a squeal of excitement from Holly. They hurry into the alcove. A most incredible sight greets them. Holly is jumping up and down in glee.

"I knew it!" she exclaims. "I saw it! I saw it..... in my dream."

The orb is back in its special place on the small cabinet in the

alcove. Its glow is brighter than they can ever remember and the

book cover vibrates in a kaleidoscope of colours. Nanna holds

her breath in amazement. When she lets go, she feels her heart

swell with love until she thinks it will burst. Grandpa struggles to

comprehend. He turns to Amanda and explains about the police,

the robbery and that not more than twenty minutes ago the orb

was not there. Holly and Nanna embrace and twirl around. The

orb has come back. They can't stop smiling and they are sure that

the orb smiles with them. How had it got there? Grandpa

interrupts their dance. A page is turning. They watch expectantly.

"Matter is energy in varying forms.

It easily transforms, transports and reforms."

They allow the words to sink in, not really sure they fully

understand them. Grandpa suggests breakfast might be a good

idea, especially as they're sure to be, unless he's mistaken,

inundated with reporters.

The reporters arrive soon after breakfast. Holly and Amanda remain upstairs while Nanna and Grandpa meet them outside the house. The reporters bombard them with questions. Do they have any ideas? Has anyone been in contact? Have they heard from the government? What do they think will happen next?

Nanna and Grandpa assure them that they had no idea that the orb had been stolen until the police woke them at five thirty, to check that they didn't have it. No-one else has contacted them, certainly not the government. It is hard to conceal their happiness and the reporters express their surprise that they are not unduly upset by the news. Nanna smiles brilliantly and reminds them of the orb's words.

"Believe in miracles."

When the reporters finally leave, they burst out laughing and rejoin Holly and Amanda in the lounge. They feel like two naughty children who've just got away with some mischief. They know they'll have to face up to the authorities soon with the fact that somehow the orb has been returned to them but for the moment their hearts are light and carefree. It's as if they are in the eye of the storm and they enjoy the calm.

Inside the house the orb sits peacefully and brilliantly in its usual place. Outside the day is perfect; bright sun in a cloudless sky. The garden sparkles and birds sing. Time and space stand still.

As the day continues, the search for the orb intensifies. Numerous sightings are reported and investigated. The theft dominates the news and is the central topic of conversation throughout the country and overseas.

Nanna and Grandpa evade further inquiries by going home with Holly and Amanda. On their way, they discuss their next move; how long they should wait before revealing the location of the orb, what explanation they could give. They decide to wait for a sign from the orb.

They return later in the evening. Nanna Em is relieved to find the orb still safely in place. She half expected it to have disappeared again. She and Grandpa stand before it for some time, each asking silent questions about its future. The book remains peacefully still, the colours on its cover gently pulsating. Finally they say goodnight and go to bed.

That night Nanna dreams she is standing with Holly on a large stage before a huge crowd in a vast concert hall. The orb is on a podium in front of them. Rows and rows of faces stare up at the stage. Questions come at Holly from all parts of the hall. She recognizes three people in the front row, the local Member of Parliament, Damian Carver, the priest, Father Diavola and the man in grey, Mr Ryman. The grey man catches her eye. His smiling face fills her vision until she is drawn into the liquid deep depths of his pupils. She wakes quickly, the dream still vivid in her memory. She knows what they have to do. She thinks about the implications for a while before falling back into a deep and peaceful sleep.

Next morning she slips downstairs to see the orb before waking Grandpa. The book is open; its message clear.

"Shoulder your responsibilities with joy."

She smiles and nods and moves into her office and fires up her computer. After some web surfing, she sits back stunned. She has recognised the hall she saw in her dream, Hamer Hall, part of the Melbourne Arts Centre Complex. She quickly downloads and prints some information and contact numbers and then heads back upstairs to wake her husband.

It's still dark and he's surprised to find her up before him. He starts to ask questions but she suggests he waits until they go on their walk with Champ and Curly.

During the walk she describes her dream and outlines what she thinks they have to do.

"Are you sure? Hire Hamer Hall?" He can't believe what he's hearing. He's most concerned about the financial ramifications. Nanna is positive. She convinces him that ticket sales will not be a problem.

After breakfast, Nanna phones Holly. Once she has told her about her dream, she outlines her plan. Holly needs no persuading. Nanna waits while she consults her mother. Amanda is less than enthusiastic, mainly concerned about Holly's safety. Nanna

175

assures her that they'll have venue security to cover the risks. Still

doubtful, Amanda relays the conversation to Matthew.

Surprisingly, he is very supportive. He starts listing people who

can help. He tells her to leave it to him.

Amanda passes on his message to Nanna who is absolutely

delighted and happy to leave it in his hands. Grandpa offers to

contact Damian Carver. They discuss possible dates and hang up.

Like a child with a new toy, Matthew leaps into action, utilizing

all the skills and contacts he has acquired in his professional life.

He finds a friend with an associate at Hamer Hall and as luck has

it, there is, unbelievably, one vacancy, an evening, in two days

time. His contact agrees to be responsible for the advertising.

He's convinced that with the public's response to the orb, the

current media coverage and the power of social media that tickets

will sell like wildfire. Matthew confirms the booking and accepts

his offer. He texts Nanna to let her know. The ball is rolling.

Grandpa contacts Damian Carver and assures him that they'll

produce the orb, if he follows their instructions. He's to issue an invitation to leaders of the government and local communities, church groups and scientists and directors of other major organizations who have shown an interest in it, to attend a special forum at Hamer Hall in two days time. Carver demands more information but once he realizes this is his only option, he grudgingly agrees to cooperate. Grandpa also requests that he makes sure that Father Diavola and Mr Ryman are there. He then promises to provide more details as soon as he has them.

The Hamer Hall contact man immediately organizes radio, television and social media coverage, advertising the proposed event. The media is delighted and leaps into action. The internet message networks go viral. Despite the short notice, all parties amazingly are able to attend. Tickets for the public sell out within half an hour of opening.

The scene is set. Within two days Holly and the orb will face them.

Unnerved by the speed at which everything is happening, Nanna asks the orb if they're doing the right thing. The orb sparkles and flips through its pages.

"All is one.

Listen to your heart.

Know and speak the truth that is there."

She knows they are leaving the calm of the eye and re-entering the storm. She trusts that Holly can handle it.

Chapter 15

The next two days fly. They all keep as low a profile as possible in the midst of phone calls, texts and newspaper and television investigations and speculation. Matthew carefully manages the booking arrangements and security for the evening and discusses the details with the Hamer Hall management team. He is satisfied that everything seems to be in order. The family is to meet with the stage and lighting technicians and staff manager in the afternoon prior to the event to run through the organisation details.

Nanna and Grandpa decide it will be easier if they stay with the family the evening before the event. They'll need to work out a plan for Holly even though she appears unconcerned by it all. Throughout all of this the orb sits peacefully in its place in the alcove. Its colours flow in rainbow patterns. The book remains closed.

When it's time to leave, Nanna carefully wraps it in its box and stows it securely in the car, while Grandpa takes Champ and Curly to a friend's place. She can feel the momentum gathering.

Holly moves through the days as if she's floating in a haze. She feels light and confident. Nothing fazes her. She has complete faith in the orb and the role she is playing….. she just wants to 'play it by ear'….. as long as Nanna is there beside her. Her parents shake their heads in despair and give up trying to have a conversation with her. Carla and Max keep out of her way. When her grandparents arrive, Holly smiles serenely and tells them it's all sorted. Nanna insists on at least discussing the practicalities of who'll be responsible for what and an outline of a strategy. Holly reluctantly acquiesces.

After dinner, Nanna produces the orb and sits it in the centre of the family room table where they gather around it. The rainbow colours flow in and out of the book. A gentle hum emanates from it. Holly feels herself being drawn back through the haze, into the present moment. She blinks and re-focusses. Six pairs of intense eyes examine her. She studies each of them in turn.

"Is there a problem?" she asks innocently. Max punches her on the arm. Carla gives a huge sigh. Her mother laughs.

"Not now. Welcome back...... I'll let Dad fill you in."

Her husband gives a brief outline of all the measures in place. He then explains their safety concerns and the need to formulate a plan of action for the presentation. If they all go in the family wagon, they can park at a friend's place in a nearby Southgate apartment block and walk to the stage door entrance of Hamer Hall. Nanna and Holly will be on stage and he and Grandpa will be in the wings in case of trouble, while Mum, Max and Carla will sit in the choir stalls.

As Holly listens carefully, she has a quick mental image of their early morning sessions with the orb. She suggests that Nanna introduces her and the orb and takes control of things, rather like their morning gatherings. Nanna agrees it's a good idea. They decide they'll work out the rest during their pre-event meeting in Hamer Hall.

Then it's early to bed for everyone. Only Holly sleeps well.

The morning starts like any other day. The family has breakfast together. It is one of those strange days when the sun rises in a blaze of red behind a bank of deep purple clouds. Rays of sunlight break through the clouds, streaming into the family room and bathing them in a crimson glow, as they review the plan for the day's activities. There is a sense of excitement and anticipation in the air. It reminds Nanna of the old saying…. 'Red sky in the morning, shepherds' warning'. She shivers and looks at the orb. It glows with a new intensity. Holly catches her reaction and follows her line of vision.

The orb trembles and the hum pulsates. The glow becomes bluer and brighter as the internal mist flows in and out of the book. The cover opens and pages turn forwards and back. The movement attracts everyone's attention as a pages settles,

"Trust that the time is right."

and then turns again.

"Go with the flow."

As they contemplate the words a deeper rose glow spreads from the orb and envelopes them. They feel its warmth and love. They high five each other. The die is cast.

The meeting at Hamer Hall goes smoothly. The manager shows them how to enter and leave by the stage door and where each of them will be. He re-assures Matthew that there will be plenty of security and the ushers will seat the audience and control question time. Those with special invitations, including Damian Carver, Father Diavola and Mr Ryman will have seats in the front row. The manager introduces them to the lighting technicians who strategically align the spotlights so that they will illuminate Holly and the orb. A special stand is produced, for the orb. Holly makes sure it's steady and secure. Two fixed microphones are set up either side of the stand and tested. There are also extra hand mikes for audience questions. They have a short practice with everyone in their place. The manager waits in the wings with Matthew and Grandpa. Amanda, Carla and Max watch from the choir stalls as Holly and Nanna position themselves either side of the stand and gaze in awe at the vast expanse of the theatre. Even with the beautiful hanging lights turned off it's an impressive sight. The two upper levels stretch into the shadows.

"It's soooo big." Holly's whisper reverberates around the hall. She jumps in surprise. The microphone is still on. Nanna nods. It's even bigger than she thought but tonight the lights will be on the stage more than the audience so hopefully it will be less intimidating.

The Show starts at seven so they promise the manager that they'll be back by six and yes, they'll remember to bring the orb. He in turn promises to meet them at the stage door entrance.

Nanna wraps the orb carefully and packs it into a large hand bag. Holly nervously watches. Matthew insists that they leave early enough to park in the Southgate Apartment car park, long before any crowds gather. He has the key to the apartment so they can pass the time there. At five to six, they casually walk from the apartment to the stage door. They are relieved to find the manager waiting for them. He greets them warmly and re-assures them that everything is under control. The crowd is already arriving outside.

The auditorium lights are on and the stage is in darkness. They watch from the wings as the seats gradually fill. Holly restlessly moves back and forth. Her parents anxiously watch her but she assures them she's fine. Nanna holds the orb.

Suddenly the auditorium is full. There is an excited buzz of conversation from the audience. Grandpa spots Damian Carver, Father Diavola and Mr Ryman sitting in the front row. He points them out to Nanna. She nods. Suddenly the lights dim slightly and the spotlights light up the empty stand at the centre of the stage. Amanda, Carla and Max quickly give Holly and Nanna a hug and kiss and wish them good luck before they take their positions in the choir stalls. Carla and Max give Holly the thumbs up as she waits in the wings with Nanna, Matthew and Grandpa.

Nanna gives Holly the orb and they walk out onto the stage. There is instant silence. It is the longest walk of Holly's life. She feels all eyes turn expectantly towards her. The orb is heavy in its bag. She positions herself next to the stand while Nanna takes her microphone. A low murmur starts to grow and resonate around the hall. Nanna hold up her hand for silence. The murmur subsides. She thanks the audience for coming and seamlessly leads them, hypnotically, into a brief meditation.

The audience and staff are so focussed that only the grey man notices Holly take the orb out of the bag and place it on the stand. When Nanna brings them back to the present there is a common gasp of wonder which grows louder and louder as the orb puts on a display. Purple lights flow through it and around it. A soft green mist rises from it and gently flows around Holly and Nanna and then weaves its way through the audience.

To Holly it's like a dream. She feels like she's floating through a mist. Before her is a sea of faces waxing and waning as if with the tide. She vaguely remembers leaving her father and Grandpa while she and Nanna walk on to the stage. She remembers the silence. The faces before her are a blur. Nanna's voice is soothing as she guides the audience in a meditation. Now the clamour of voices seems to come from a distance.

She focusses her attention on the front row and recognizes Damian Carver, Father Diavola and the grey man about whom they still know nothing. The minister for science is also there. 'Mr Reeman with a y catches', her eye and for a second she is drawn into his depths. He smiles and nods.

In an instant the mist clears and she is sharply aware of her surroundings, every detail now clearly etched. The auditorium is packed on all levels. People stand along the walls. Television cameras are angled towards them. A large screen is suspended above the stage. Nanna is standing waiting at the microphone and the orb…. the orb is putting on a display.

The clamour of voices fades into a collective sigh from the audience. This is what they've come to see. Holly takes a deep breath and whispers a plea for help. Then she stands tall and as Nanna steps back, she moves to her microphone, welcomes them all and thanks them for coming. Her voice, a mere whisper carries clearly. The orb settles into a soft mauve mist. Holly explains that she has no idea of what the outcome will be but that she hopes she can show them that the orb is what it is and not some trick or fraud. When she describes how the orb works, a murmur of scepticism ripples through part of the audience. It triggers a thought in Holly's head. She singles out the minister for science and asks him to choose someone to join her on stage to bear witness to what might happen. He hurriedly consults with Damian Carver and Father Diavola who immediately turn and point to the grey man. He nods and stands to face the audience. Holly asks the audience if they are happy with the choice. Agreement is unanimous and he joins her and Nanna on stage. Holly invites him to take charge of the proceedings. He hesitates and then calls upon the audience for questions.

Over two thousand voices respond, hurling questions onto the stage, some heartfelt, some condemning, some acerbic and some genuinely inquiring. As Holly steps back from the onslaught the orb's aura intensifies and vibrant blue rays of light blaze across the auditorium.

The barrage immediately ceases and the audience holds its breath. The light display dwindles until there is just a bright halo around the orb. As the crowd start to find its voice again, the grey man holds up his hand for order. He suggests that as individual questions are obviously impossible to cover, that Holly respond to the most common questions and accusations that have been fired at her.

In that instant the questions are clear and ordered in her mind. She knows what she has to say. The audience wants the truth so she speaks about the truth. She warns them that some might not like the truth, that some might not accept the truth, that some will not recognize the truth, that some will manipulate the truth for their own ends and that some will look into their own hearts and know the truth. The words flow easily from her as the soft mauve mist from the orb wraps itself around her.

She explains that she and the orb are just the messengers. Messengers have been sent before and only accepted by some. If the messenger was not in an expected form the message was not accepted. What is an acceptable form of messenger or message? Who amongst them is truly qualified to determine whether or not the messenger or the message is true? This inability to come to a consensus is clearly demonstrated by the debate that now raged around the orb.

However, she continues, the massive response to the orb and its messages clearly indicates that there is a great need in the world for universal guidance and direction. People want to believe. They need to believe in the truth of the orb and its messages. Therefore it is important to clear away the doubt and the accusations of fraud and profiteering.

Holly speaks clearly and briefly about how they had found the orb, how they had discovered its abilities and how things had snowballed from that point on. She outlines the events following the government's intervention. She admits she has no idea as to why she was chosen nor how the orb works. She only knows that there has to be some inner core of belief within a person, even if it wasn't a conscious one, for the orb to respond. She believes that some sectors of the community are threatened by the orb, that they feared their power may be diminished. She challenges the

authorities and organizations and church leaders who oppose the

veracity of the orb to look into their hearts and determine their

true intent and motives. She pauses for a moment as she feels an

intense wave of mixed emotions from the audience flow over her;

warmth and love, confusion and doubt, openness and hostility

mixed with anger and fear.

She allows her gaze to fix on several individuals. Then she

throws up her hands and laughs.

"See," she says. "Even now there are believers and doubters,

those with hope and those without, supporters and antagonists.

All hear the same words and see the same things but not all

perceive the same truth. The truth is inside you and that truth is

from the heart of the universe. All is one. You have the choice to

see or not see." The audience starts to clamour again.

The grey man intervenes. He calls for calm and then signals to

her to continue. Holly urges them not to judge hastily but to let

the orb respond to some of their questions. She asks the grey man

to select some individuals from the audience to come onto the

191

stage and ask a question. Hundreds of hands shoot up. The grey man carefully chooses a selection of people to represent the different sectors, sexes and age groups. Thirty are chosen including, church and community leaders, public identities, children, teenagers, parents and the aged, the minister for science and the priest. A buzz of excitement runs through the crowd as they make their way to the stage.

Holly steps back and joins Nanna, allowing the grey man to manage the show. The orb sits peacefully in its bed of light and mist.

A dropped pin could have been heard as the first person approaches the orb. Most people recognize her as an acerbic television games hostess. There is a giggle from the audience as she boldly asks if her ratings will continue to grow. A few irritated voices call out and demand serious questions but Holly smiles and shrugs and points to the orb. All eyes watch as one. Those at the back of the auditorium watch the large overhead screen. The light around the orb seems to twinkle as if in merriment. The crowd gasps as slowly the pages of the book

turn. The grey man reads clearly from the page.

"Give thanks for what you have."

Hoots of laughter and applause echo round the hall. Holly turns

to Nanna to conceal a laugh. The television hostess turns red to

the roots but is gracious enough to acknowledge the advice with a

'touché' and thank you.

The ice is broken. The crowd relaxes. The orb is magnificent.

For each question there is a significant piece of advice. Holly and

Nanna notice that each time the orb answers its light changes to a

different hue to fit the nature of the question: red for the

community, orange for relationships, yellow for the personal,

green for the heart, blue for communication, indigo for mind

matters and mauve for spiritual issues….. the colours of the

rainbow! For the purest of questioners, it glows a brilliant white.

Finally there are only three of the thirty left in the line; the

minister of science, a cynical radio personality and Father

Diavola. The parliamentarian comes first. He addressed the audience rather than the orb.

'What is truth?'

There are sniggers in the audience. The orb's glow became a radiant white as its pages turned. The grey man reads its reply.

"Truth is the purity within the heart of your heart.

Peel away the layers and look into your heart.

Search within."

There are several snide comments from the audience about politicians not having hearts.

Another page rapidly turns and the grey man hides a smile as he relays the message.

"Believe in miracles!"

Even the MP laughs and he gives a mock bow to the audience before leaving the stage. They clap as he leaves.

The radio personality is not amused by the interplay. He strides onto the stage and demands that the orb give him proof. The orb's glow gradually fades until it totally disappears. The book remains open at its previous page.

'Believe in miracles.'

Everyone waits. The silence stretches and become awkward. The orb hasn't refused to answer any other questions. The radio man turns and glares accusingly at Holly and Nanna. They just smile and shrug. He gives a snort of contempt and flounces off the stage.

The book closes and the orb emits a gentle glow.

The final questioner is the priest Father Diavola. Holly and Nanna study him carefully as he approaches the orb. He stops a few paces away from it and turns to face them. They feel his fear and pain. His face is etched in stone, stern and sombre. He hurls his question at Holly before turning and repeating it to the orb.

'Are you working with the devil or are you a witch?'

Holly and Nanna step back aghast. Holly feels a tremor pass through her body. Nanna wraps an arm around her. The audience gasp and sit up. The grey man tenses and studies the priest's face for a moment before returning his attention to the orb.

The priest's face is impenetrable. The auditorium is hushed in expectation. How will the orb answer?

A ripple of light runs through the orb from red through the colours of the rainbow to a brilliant white. Inside the orb the pages of the book quiver and glow gold before they start to turn quickly, one after the other. The grey man rapidly reads the messages.

"There is no hell only heaven.

Heaven is pure unconditional love.

Heaven is the state of supreme happiness.

Hell is the reflected image of your hates, angers, fears and doubts.

Evil is the manifestation of your hate, anger and fear and the negative use of power.

The orb is as one with the universe.

The universe is evolving. It is a part of eternity.

You are as a freckle on the skin of the universe.

Until all parts are one the whole cannot be perfect.

You have the means to create peace and happiness for all.

It is within each one of you.

Look for the truth within yourself.

Be compassionate.

Be loving.

Be forgiving, first to yourself and then to others.

Be free of all shackles that bind you."

Holly and Nanna are astounded by the intensity and length of the orb's response. They feel the electricity in the audience as they watch the priest's face struggle with emotions from doubt to fear to anger. He steps closer to the orb but it has not finished.

The book opens and closes in rapid succession, each time returning to the same two pages.

"Be compassionate.

Be loving.

Be forgiving, first to yourself and then to others.

Be free of all shackles that bind you.

Be compassionate.

Be loving.

Be forgiving, first to yourself and then to others.

Be free of all shackles that bind you.

Be compassionate.

Be loving.

Be forgiving, first to yourself and then to others.

Be free of all shackles that bind you."

The priest steps closer.

Suddenly the orb erupts in flashes of lightning, striking the space between it and the priest. The lights of the auditorium go out. Holly instinctively moves towards the orb which is now a pale grey ball of light. The grey man urgently indicates to her to take it and leave under the cover of darkness. Holly grabs the orb and she and Nanna rush to the wings where her father and Grandpa are waiting. They make a quick exit towards the stage door entrance. The muted glow from the orb lights their way.

In the choir stalls, Amanda, Carla and Max, using Max's phone light as a guide, escape as quickly as they can and head for the stage door. They arrive in perfect time to meet the others. Behind them pandemonium breaks loose. Faint phone lights start to appear in the hall but the stage is shrouded in total darkness.

Once outside, Matthew takes charge. He swiftly shepherds the family along Southgate Avenue, keeping to the shadows, until they reach the apartment block and their car. Within five minutes they are heading for home.

Despite their dramatic departure, they feel quite calm. They discuss the orb's reactions and ponder the consequences. The press will have a field day. How will the church respond? What will happen to the orb now?

Matthew drives slowly along the back roads to their house to make sure there are no reporters to confront them. All is quiet but Holly stops him before they pull into their drive.

She feels her heart constrict and a wave of sadness overwhelm her. She knows what they have to do.

"Dad, we have to go to Nanna's and Grandpa's," she says quietly.

Chapter 16

Her father doesn't hesitate. Within half an hour, when
they are almost there, the orb, safely cradled in Holly's lap,
changes from soft grey glow to a warm pink. It starts to hum and
the pages of the book begin to turn. Holly leans forward and taps
her father on the shoulder.

"Stop at the beach, dad." He does as she says. He parks a short
distance from the house, away from the road and prying eyes. He
turns off the headlights. Apart from the glow of the orb, they are
in darkness. Dense clouds obscure the moon and stars. The night
is still. The only sound is the gentle ebb and flow of the waves on
the sand.

The pages of the book continue to slowly turn. Finally they stop.
Inside the car, they feel an incredible peace descend upon them.
Holly lifts the orb so they can all read the book. They read it
together.

"Thank you."

Holly knows it's time to let the orb go, to return it to the universe. The others feel it too. She thinks it would be nice if the dogs were there as they'd been there at the beginning.

"I'll get the dogs." It's almost as if Grandpa is reading her thoughts. "I'll meet you on the beach."

He quietly opens all the car's doors and hurriedly makes his way to his friend's house. Max likewise closes the doors carefully when everyone's out. Holly, using the orb's glow as a light, leads them silently to the beach.

A warm mist envelops them as they pass through the bush. Halfway there, they are joined by Grandpa and the two delighted dogs. As they cross onto the sand, the moon breaks free from behind the clouds. Its pale silver light reflects in the flat, calm surface of the sea. They follow the path of its light along the sand, close to the edge of the water.

The dogs, Champ and Curly, run ahead. Suddenly they both stop and growl softly. Holly feels the orb respond. It seems to draw the moonlight into itself and out on to the beach where the dogs are waiting. She feels the pulse of it flow down her body and into the sand. The group gathers around the dogs.

An astounding sight greets them. Emerging from the sand are the same conical mounds and tree patterns they'd seen the morning the orb arrived. For Matthew and Amanda, it's their first hand experience of the realities of the magic of the orb. It's beyond belief. They stand gob smacked as the truth of it all really hits them. Grandpa wraps his arms around them.

Nanna guides them to form a circle around the largest mound, the dogs included. They stand solemn and silent.

Holly tightens her grip on the orb. She feels its warmth. She feels its love. Tears course down her face as she places it gently on the mound. Nanna kneels beside her, her hand on her shoulder.

The orb's light oscillates through the colours of the rainbow and they have the sensation that the colours flow from it through their bodies across the sand and into the circle of family. They stand and step back.

Go with love, whispers Holly and thank you. They all say their goodbyes.

The pages of the book turn one last time.

"Live in the present.

The soul of the universe is yours.

Unconditional love is the key."

The mound sinks. The grains of sand close over the orb until the beach is as it was before. For a long while they stand in silence. The clouds drift back and forth across the face of the moon, creating eerie patterns on the water and sand.

For Holly it's as if a part of her has been torn away and the threads that bind her heart have broken apart. Then she hears the words in her head...

"The presence of the universe is with you always."

.... and she remembers the words of the orb, that it belongs to the universe. She realizes that the threads are still there but stretched further and that she has only to look into her heart to reconnect.

Max hears it first, that rushing sound of a rogue wave. He yells a warning and the group breaks and rushes up the beach as the waves roll in with a series of thunderous crashes. The tension is broken. The sky is suddenly clear, filled with a multitude of stars. The moon illuminates the beach.

Hand in hand Holly, Nanna, Grandpa, Carla, Max, Amanda and Matthew retrace their steps back up through the bush to the car. The two dogs bring up the rear. Wisps of a soft green mist float lightly above them. They pile into the car, dogs and all and head for Nanna's and Grandpa's house.

When they re-enter the house Holly feels strangely lighter as if a burden has been lifted from her shoulders. She hears her sister give an exclamation of wonder. There where the orb has sat is a small book, a replica of the one inside the orb. The book sits in a warm rosy glow. Carla reverently picks it up and turns the first page. Everyone crowds around to see its words.

"Smile."

Each page contains a different message from the orb. Nanna smiles. Even though the orb is gone its words are there to remind them.

Amanda and the family decide to stay the night. They have supper on the deck and afterwards, before bed, Holly and Nanna stand for a while looking into the night sky until they became one with the universe. It's hard to believe it's barely seven weeks since the orb arrived and now it's gone.

Holly thinks back over the startling and dramatic events that have changed their lives, culminating in the return of the orb to wherever it came from. She ponders on the loss of the peaceful life she used to live. She misses the tranquillity of pre orb but regrets none of the changes it has wrought. She looks at Nanna, standing beside her and wonders if she feels the same. Nanna, as if catching her thoughts, turns to her.

"Do you think it's out there watching us?"

Chapter 17

Holly wakes with a start, caught in a recurring dream. Where is she? She recalls. It's the school holidays and she, Carla and Max are once again staying with their grandparents. She struggles to retain the dream in her memory, aware that it's the fifth time she's dreamt it. Something strikes her about the day. Images flitter in and out of her consciousness until finally they stick. Today! It is a year today! One year since finding the orb. She wonders why that's important. She focusses on her surroundings, the same grandparents and house, the same view, the same sister and brother; the same but not the same.

Even after twelve months, the controversy rages. For some, the jury is still out. The public, the media, the government, the scientists and especially the churches were and still are divided in their accounts and interpretations of the events of that last audience with the orb. The local Member of Parliament, Damian

Carver has resigned. The priest Father Diavola has entered a

closed order in a monastery and the grey man has mysteriously

vanished. There's something about the grey man she can't quite

grasp. 'Mr Reeman with a y'.

People still stop her in the street to hear her speak and seek her

advice. Her radio appearances are more popular than ever and top

the ratings. She's a regular guest at conferences and seminars and

often invited to be on television shows. Offers to travel interstate

and overseas pour in but Holly declines them all. School is the

only place she can be who she was. The novelty of her fame was

soon replaced by a new pop sensation.

Nanna has stepped back from the limelight. She steadfastly

supports Holly from the sidelines, offering advice and counsel

when she thinks it's required. Nanna's meditation, reiki and

hypnosis practice has blossomed. The family sometimes grumbles

a little about the reduced time available for them and the dogs eye

her soulfully every time she misses a walk.

Despite the whirlwind, she manages to maintain her inner calm.

She consciously practices the teachings of the orb. She refers to

the book, left behind by the orb, using its words of advice as a

supplement for her inner knowledge. The book, perpetually

encased in a warm coloured glow, continues to sit on the cabinet

in the alcove in Nanna's house.

Images from the dream return. In it she is following a path

through a beautiful garden. The path meanders through botanic

rooms, each a colour of the rainbow, each with quiet sanctuaries

where one can sit and relax and be soothed by the sound of gently

flowing water. At the end of the path is a simple, contemporary

sandstone building set amongst vivid white flowers, peaceful

ponds and a raked crystal garden. Inside the building a central

chamber is filled with a radiant white light, its source a pyramid

of glassed roof. The inner walls are dressed alpine ash and the

floor polished white marble. White soft cushioned seats are

placed against the walls and in a small alcove set into one of the

walls is a beautiful leadlight cabinet.

On the cabinet sits her book. Radiating from the chamber are other rooms, each with a different colour scheme and a beautiful garden view. One is prepared for healing, another for meditation and relaxation and another for listening to music. Despite the absolute peace that surrounds the gardens and building, she feels something is missing. There is a strange feeling of expectancy, as if the gardens and building are waiting for something. Is it her?

She comes back to the present. Today is a quiet day in her busy schedule so she and Nanna, Grandpa, Carla, Max and the dogs are able to take a leisurely walk along the beach. The sand has finally recovered from the frenzied digging that had taken place after the news that they had returned the orb to its origins. No amount of digging had turned up any clues. Some people still believe that the orb is hidden somewhere. Some consider it all a publicity stunt thought up by the media. Many are undecided. Fortunately they still have the original photos they had taken that day one year ago.

This morning, the only reminder of that morning, are wisps of a soft mist that drift down the track and follow them onto the beach.

As they walk, Holly describes her dream to the others. They try to interpret its message. Immersed in their discussions, they almost collide with another walker. They apologize and look about them. There are quite a few people on the beach. Holly is surprised because they usually have it to themselves at this hour. Then it strikes her. People! That was it! There were no people in the dream. The garden and building are waiting for people. She turns excitedly to her grandparents. We've got to build it! Some how we've got to build a peace garden - a rainbow garden of peace where anyone can visit. Holly is very excited and more animated than her grandparents or siblings have ever seen her. The plans spill out of her. The design is there in her head. They must create it just like the garden and building in her dream. Somehow they will find the means. They can start by directing all the media monies she receives into a Peace Garden Fund. The rest will come from somewhere.

Her grandparents and Carla enthusiastically join in the discussion. The vision expands.

Meanwhile Max has wandered back along the beach, the dogs at his heels. He stops, puzzled and stands and stares for a moment at the retreating back of the man with whom they had nearly collided. He tries to catch up with him but no matter how fast he moves, the gap remains the same. Frustrated he returns to the others a strange expression on his face.

"What's up Max?'" Carla has been observing him.

Max frowns. "I'm not positive but I think that was the grey man. You know, the man who took the orb, the man on the stage."

Holly looks startled.

"Mr Reeman with a y?"

"Yeh," replies Max. "That's him."

They all turn to look but there is no sign of the grey man.

EPILOGUE

Five years later, unheralded by media fanfare, Holly opened her first Peace Garden. A small gathering of family, close friends and helpers celebrated the occasion. As she guided the group through the gardens and the building, Holly could hardly believe they had accomplished so much. Where had the time come from? How had they managed it all?

She thought back to when she'd first had the dream and that morning on the beach when she'd realized what she had to do. It was incredible how opportunity had fallen into her lap, how her life had led her to architecture and landscape design.

Just as she had embarked on the project, a noted book publisher had invited her to tell the story of the orb. With remarkable speed the book was written, printed and launched to become such an overnight sensation that several quick reprints were required. Its success brought about an incredible offer to produce a film. This in turn broke all box-office records.

All monies from the book and film were channelled into a Peace Garden Trust Fund. She managed to keep her involvement with the garden private. A special committee of family and their closest friends was established to manage the trust fund. Her mother was chosen to head the Trust. It was vital to maintain the integrity of the venture. The Peace Garden had to be a place of peace not a tourist amusement park. Gradually, by word of mouth, people would discover the garden and share in its gift, its life.

All this time the garden was developing. Once Holly had sketched the images from the dream and they had found the land, her father had directed the project. The son of their closest friends, a graduate architect, helped with the design of the building. A builder friend carried out the construction. They asked a young couple, who ran a local nursery, to assist with the landscaping and plants. Gradually the Peace Garden grew until it became one with the vivid memory of Holly's dream.

Two nights ago the dream had come again; this time with a difference. This time there were people walking in the garden or resting on seats in the sheltered arbours. The different sections of the garden featured masses of plants reflecting the colours of the rainbow. Within the various rooms of the building people were listening to music, reading, meditating and healing. The place was alive. She could feel its serene heart beating. She felt it again today, a warm peaceful sanctuary. She felt its life.

Standing now in the central chamber of the building, illuminated by the incandescent white light, Holly marvelled at its overall beauty and serenity. It was a miracle. The dream was a reality. You just had to believe. Set back in one of the walls was a small alcove. In the alcove, on a simple cabinet, lit by the white light, sat her copy of the book from within the orb. Its cover shimmered with a vibrant pink, violet and white. She still used it regularly. It was like a friend. Facsimiles of the small book, in which were written the messages from the orb, were sold with her book.

Standing beside the cabinet, she looked across at her family, and the friends and helpers who were gathered about her and felt a warm wave of love flood through her. Her grandparents were just as fit and healthy as they had been five years ago, Nanna as usual radiating calm. Carla had just returned from volunteering abroad, working for the 'Save the Children Foundation'. Max had become immersed in Quantum Physics and the sciences of possibility. Her parents were her pillars of strength, managing the practicalities of her life.

Just as she was about to thank them all for their help and support, a man in a grey suit stepped out of the group and moved towards her. She recognised him instantly. She opened her mouth to speak but no words emerged. He smiled kindly and presented her with a beautifully wrapped box. Her hands seemed to move of their own accord as she graciously accepted it. The grey man stepped back. Only Nanna witnessed him melt into the crowd.

Everyone watched entranced as Holly carefully unwrapped the present. Tears welled in her eyes. There seated on a bed of wool was the orb. Or was it the orb? It glowed like the orb. She gently lifted it out of the box for all to see. There was a collective gasp. The orb sparkled. Everyone gathered closer. Holly examined it from all angles. The only difference appeared to be that there was no book inside it. Holly placed the orb next to the book. It settled into place just like the original orb, quite at home. The white light from the roof above sent thousands of refracted coloured beams across the room. From the orb flowed a peaceful light. Holly turned to look for the man but he was gone. She looked at Nanna who just smiled and nodded.

Then she paid tribute to the orb for all it had brought and would bring for themselves and many others. As she finished, a page of the book turned. They all watched in wonder, their breaths held in anticipation. It had not turned of its own accord for six years.

They had forgotten how it made them feel. As one they stretched forward to read its message.

"Believe in miracles."

The garden is a sanctuary of love and peace, the orb and its book a symbol of hope and guidance for the future. Hundreds and thousands of pilgrims visit the garden every year.

Acknowledgements

My sincere thanks go to my husband Rob, my special friend Norma and my daughter Jacquie for their encouragement and support and for reading and making suggestions as the story evolved. Thank you too to our friend Graham whose proof reading discovered quite a few errors.

Thank you to my 'Insight Timer' followers who have enjoyed and written such great reviews about my meditations featuring 'The Orb'. I hope you will enjoy the full story.

Finally, but not least, thank you to all the readers who have been prepared to read my story.

About Estelle Godsman

Estelle Godsman is a retired teacher. She lives with her husband and two dogs on the beautiful Mornington Peninsula. Her three daughters, grandchildren, daughter-in-law and sons-in-law help keep her in touch with the modern world.

Since retiring she has immersed herself in studying hypnosis and practising and teaching painting, reiki and meditation.

It's her belief that in the current rush and madness of the world, we need some gentler hidden messages to present to our readers, especially our children, that offer guidance on how to live in peace and harmony. This conviction has guided her to write the Orb. Its hero is a girl. The characters are ordinary, real life and present day. The elements of mystery, drama and magic are used as a canvas on which to interweave positive behaviour patterns and attitudes to help us handle the increasing pressures and stresses of our world. Our subconscious minds, where our patterns of behaviour are set, respond positively to the use of the imagination and metaphor. This is rather like the tales of old.

'The Orb' is a work of fiction. Characters, institutions and organisations mentioned in this novel are either the product of the author's imagination or, if real, used fictitiously without any intent to describe actual conduct.

154	146	143
86	88	87
79	77	76

Made in the USA
Monee, IL
19 October 2020